What if?

Eleven: 1

For more information, to inquire about rights to this or other works, or to purchase copies for special educational, business, or sales promotional uses please write to:

Tedeschi Publishing
294 S. Cedar Ave.
Wood Dale, Il 60191
Vickivass.com

FIRST EDITION

Published in Print and Digital formats in the United States of America

ISBN: 13: 978-0692771969

Eleven: 1

Victoria Vass

Tedeschi Publishing
Chicago, Illinois

To Vicki's father, Charles Vass, the smartest man she knew; and to Brian's father, Tony Tedeschi, who taught him what it is to be a man; and to our son Tony, who reminds us what it means to stay a boy.

Eleven: 1

Now the whole world had one language and a common speech.
-- Genesis 11:1

Agunwi Village, Sudan, Africa

Alexander's head ached from the sorghum grain alcohol. It was the native drink of the Agunwi tribe, a home brew made from their only harvested crop. To refuse it would have been an insult to his native hosts, so he downed it with a smile and a shrug.

Last time he had drunk this much he was a grad student at the University of Illinois. To think of it, the alcohol wasn't that much better then, either. Except instead of native drums he would have been listening to John Hiatt.

The U of I and John Hiatt were worlds away from this remote village in the heart of southern Sudan, Africa's largest country. Southern Sudan was a vast savanna with little but meadow grass and trees; the Blue Nile that bordered the village was dirty and not much more than a creek. There was little civilization—no Internet, no electricity, no phone lines. Even the roads were trails carved out by villagers walking from one village to the next or the utility vehicles driven by the relief workers.

Alexander was willing to put up with the discomfort for the sake of his studies. In the span of three days he had learned more about the Agunwi than he could have garnered from any textbook that he had read in graduate school. Alexander ran a hand through his tousled black hair. His skin was the palest among these natives, and his blue eyes were a source of curiosity to the villagers. Most of them had never seen a white man before. Even under the layers of African dirt, Alexander's handsome features were apparent. His chiseled good looks would probably seem more at home at a country club than here.

To look at him now, it was hard to imagine him as a sickly kid holed up in his room with his nose in a book. As a child he dreamed of adventures like this. The world came alive through the words of Kipling, Stevenson, and his favorite book, *Swiss Family Robinson*. Alexander's father gave him that book when he was eight. His father was a career soldier and hardly ever home, but when he was, every minute was an adventure. They built their own awesome tree house and fought pirates as fierce as those the Robinsons defeated.

He and his father would sit around the campfire and tell stories all night long. Now Alexander's father was in Washington, DC, and he couldn't remember the last time he had seen him. He longed for those innocent days when they would sit around the campfire until the sun appeared.

This campfire's glow was the only refuge from the complete darkness of the bush. The stories and drums would continue throughout the night, but Alexander wouldn't last much longer. He was exhausted after spending the day walking from village to village, sometimes miles under the heat of the unforgiving sun.

"Catch ya later," he told his new frat brothers as he stood up, stretching his legs. The common phrase from home had become a joke to the locals, as they didn't have any hard *K* sounds in their language. As much as Alexander tried, he couldn't get them to pronounce this consonant correctly.

He went off to the solace of his tent, taking care to check the area and his sleeping bag for unwanted critters. Even though the night was humid, he left his layers on for protection. Sudan's dry season was like the worst August day in Chicago. A line from a John Hiatt song played through his head: "It was so humid the moon began to sweat." It was probably around 100 degrees with equal humidity and no chance of escaping to a swimming pool or an air-conditioned room.

Sleeping required ten percent determination and ninety percent grain alcohol. Although Alexander had bathed before going to bed in water that had been boiled, his khakis and Fighting Illini t-shirt clung to him, and he was covered with the gritty dust that caked over everything.

Bathing here was a chore, but his guide Amat insisted on wiping off the dust and germs from the eternal friendliness of the villagers. Each time Alexander stepped out of his tent, the villagers crowded around him. They all wanted to shake his hand. Alexander obliged them but was careful to wash frequently.

To bathe, Alexander had the village women boil water. He then mixed the boiled purified water with cooler purified water, so as not to burn his skin. There was no shower; he literally just poured water over his head. He never felt completely clean. Tonight was no exception.

He longed for sleep. Throughout his days here, he had found sleep a long time in coming, but tonight he knew that it would not be a problem; it was his last night in this particular village. His going-away party would be an all-nighter for the Agunwi.

The drums faded as he closed his eyes. The buzz of mosquitoes around the netting that surrounded him comforted him in its familiarity. Little comforted him in this dark, brooding place.

Glasgow, Scotland

Clutching her briefcase, Rebekah strode down the tree-lined streets of the University of Glasgow. In the four years she had lived in Scotland, she had grown to love the university and the surrounding countryside. It was rich in history and in beauty. She had attained a slight Scottish brogue, but her Yankee tenacity revealed her country of origin. Though reluctant at first, the Scots had welcomed her as one of their own as she won them over with her beauty and wit and her willingness to embrace local customs.

Looking up as she walked, she saw the tall spires of the old Main Building rising up over the hills. It dated back 550 years to when the English ruled Scotland. She wasn't quite that old, but sometimes she felt as if she had lived that long. She stopped and stared at the cool gray stone exterior of the tower and marveled at how far she had traveled to get where she was. Not just in miles, but in life. The tragedy of the past had put her at a crossroads. She had been nine on the day that changed her life forever.

***

It was a fall day and the Michigan Wolverines had just won their homecoming game. Mr. and Mrs. Simmonds never missed a Wolverines game. Tony was a professor of history at the U of M in Ann Arbor, and Margaret was a professor of philosophy. The two had met at a football game while graduate students. A year later, Rebekah, or Becky as her parents called her, was born.

They showered her with love and attention and food. She was raised in the era when the four main food groups were starches, red meat, whole milk, and Twinkies. Her mom would say, "It's baby fat. You'll lose it when you become a teenager." Maybe she did lose the external fat, but she would never lose the fat girl inside her. She had built a wall around herself to keep people out.

She never quite fit in at school, so she spent most of her time on the U of M campus and felt more comfortable talking with grad students about Descartes than she did with nine-year-old girls. Being a girl and fat in the fourth grade was a ticket to Loserville. Becky opted for a different train ride. She went the way of books and solitude. She didn't care about makeup, boys, or clothes. In her heart she hoped that someday genetics would kick in and she would become the beautiful woman that her mother was.

Her parents never said no to her so when she whined about stopping for ice cream on the way home from the homecoming game, they stopped at the Baskin Robbins a block away from their house. While her parents ordered, Becky went to use the washroom. She dawdled in the washroom looking at herself in the mirror. She sucked in her stomach so her developing boobs would stick out further. The only benefit to being fat was that your boobs looked bigger than most nine year olds.

When she first heard the sound of explosions echoing, she had thought it was fireworks, possibly a late homecoming celebration. But when she heard the screams and thuds and breaking glass, she knew it was something much worse. Rebekah's knees buckled and she slumped to the floor, hovering against the wall between the toilet and the window. Her teeth chattered. She couldn't move. She heard footsteps along the hallway. Someone paused outside the door to the bathroom and jiggled the knob. Rebekah wrapped her arms tighter around herself. She felt a warmth trickling down her legs to the floor.

She hid there frozen for what seemed longer than the ten minutes it actually took the police to arrive. She heard the sirens sounding their shrill scream into the still fall night and then the approaching squawks of the police's two-way radios. At the sound of the siren, whoever had been fiddling with the door took off. With all the excitement, Rebekah had forgotten the reason she had come into the bathroom in the first place. Now it was too late. She was embarrassed and didn't want the police to see that she had wet herself.

She heard the rush of loud, official-sounding voices. She listened for her parents' voices in the commotion but could not make them out. The bathroom door burst open. On the other side was a cop brandishing a gun. When he saw her, he put his gun down and called to someone behind him.

A young officer had come and led her out. Perez was his name. Rebekah remembered reading his silver badge. He had tried to shield her from the devastation, but not in time. She saw the splatters of blood, a red pool mixing with a runny chocolate one. She recognized the ring on the finger of the hand that had been holding the cone. She stopped and stared. She didn't recognize anything other than the ring and the blue and white scarf her mother always wore on game day. Lying next to her was her dad—a great big athlete of a man—lifeless, brought down by a single bullet. The fat girl died that day.

"Daddy," she murmured as the tears welled and her throat closed up. Perez led her out to a squad car. The robber had stolen eighty-six dollars in cash and Rebekah's childhood that night.

From then on it had been an endless series of foster homes and "what ifs." What if the game hadn't gone into overtime? What if they'd had a flat tire? What if she hadn't insisted on stopping for an ice cream cone? What if her parents had said no? What if? What if? What if? It was a never-ending refrain in her head.

When she found religion couldn't provide the answers to her questions, she turned to books. She would escape from a foster home and scour the rows of books in the local library. That's how, years later, she stumbled across Professor Angus McLean's book, *Principles of Chaotic Math.* In this one volume she found the key to understanding "what ifs." Chaotic math became her talisman against the violent randomness that happens. It's not God. It's not the devil. It's not nature. It's not nurture. It just is. Randomness just is. She learned what ifs could sometimes be explained. She was seventeen years old.

***

Here she was now, twenty-six years old and about to preach the gospel of chaotic math to a lecture room full of freshmen. Her mom would be proud to see that genetics had kicked in with a vengeance. She had turned into a beautiful young woman who was late for her first day of lectures. She made the hall in time to hear Professor Anne Knuth introduce her. She stepped up to the podium and saw a roomful of kids no more than four years her junior. She froze and took a sip of water. Then she began.

She took a quarter from her pocket and threw it to a handsome young man in the front row. He looked surprised but caught it.

"Without opening your hand, tell me: is it heads or tails?" Rebekah asked.

The boy thought for a moment and said, "Heads."

"What is the chance that you are right?"

"Well, fifty-fifty. It could be heads or tails."

"So if you flip a coin ten times, it will come up heads five times and tails five times?" Rebekah asked.

"Well, I don't know." The boy studied the quarter in his palm. "There's only two sides. So if one side has to face up, wouldn't that mean I have a one out of two chances of being right?"

"Open your hand," Rebekah said.

He did and glanced down at the coin. "It's tails," the boy replied.

"This is a common fallacy about randomness. It's called the Monte Carlo theory. Just because you flip a coin ten times and heads appears five times does not hedge your bet that the sixth time will be tails. Each flip is a new and unique event. It is not predetermined by the previous events, or is it? I ask you now to ask yourself the first question in chaotic math: what if?"

Agunwi village, Sudan, Africa

The buzzing grew louder in Alexander's ear. It was too loud for a mosquito, he thought. His head ached, and his face felt numb. With a hand shaky from too much alcohol, he reached up to his forehead. Something moved under his fingers. He jumped out of bed, tangled in the mosquito netting, still grasping the thrashing beetle. His first impulse was to throw it to the ground and smash it. But he stopped when he saw the brilliant colors of the bug. His intellectual curiosity kicked in. It was like nothing he had seen before in a textbook or in the field. He grabbed an empty Mason jar that he kept by the air mattress for midnight emergencies. He put the bug in the jar and closed the lid. Grabbing his pocketknife, he poked holes in the top.

Carrying the jar, Alexander walked the few feet to Amat's tent. A patient and proud African, Amat, had been his tour guide for this trip. He was a fellow professor at the University of Nairobi.

"Amat," Alexander called into his tent.

"Over here," Amat called, walking up behind Alexander. He was carrying a fish that he had caught in the Nile, which was only a short walk away. Amat thought the best fishing was in the predawn hours.

"Is this poisonous?" Alexander held up the Mason jar, showing him the still thrashing beetle.

"I've never seen that before," Amat said, peering into the jar. "Where did you find it?"

"It found my face while I was sleeping."

"Have you talked to Methu yet?"

Methu was the village medicine man who lived in the mud hut on the edge of the village. At ninety-eight years old Methu had far outlived the average span of the Agunwi. He looked like a walking beef jerky. He held the knowledge of all the generations of Agunwi. Not having any written language, he was the keeper of their stories.

Alexander had an audience with Methu when he had first arrived in the village but couldn't get much information. As friendly as these people were, they were very wary of strangers. Alexander followed Amat toward Methu's hut. A crowd of local children quickly followed behind, chattering loudly.

Hearing their voices, Methu came out of his mud hut wearing the Chicago Bulls t-shirt that Alexander had given him during his ceremonial visit with the elder. Alexander hadn't seen him since that initial visit.

Methu sank onto an antelope skin, crossing his long legs. He motioned for Alexander and Amat to sit on the skin across from him. After what seemed like hours of pleasantries, Alexander was finally able to get to the point of his visit. At this point, it was already late afternoon. He pulled the jar out of his backpack.

Methu motioned for Alexander to pass the jar to him. He studied it, smiling a toothless grin and rubbing his head. "I haven't seen this since I was a young boy," Methu said in stilted English.

Alexander got excited. "You've seen it? What do you call it? Is it poisonous?" He rattled off questions.

Amat held out his hand to the excited American. "Slow down; one question at a time, my friend."

The medicine man's English was limited, so Amat translated as the old man spoke quickly. "It's a kula." At Alexander's confused expression, Amat explained for the medicine man. "A rain beetle. They live very deep within the ground and only come out when there is much rain."

"Huh? There's no rain now," Alexander said. "What did you call it?"

"A kula."

Alexander's brow wrinkled in confusion. Amat looked confused as well. "I thought you had no 'k' sound," Alexander said.

"We didn't name it. My grandfather told me what it was." Amat translated the old man's words.

"Where'd your grandfather hear about it?" Amat asked for Alexander.

"The Valley of the Voices."

"Do you know where that is?" Alexander asked Amat.

"I think he is referring to a valley through the pass of the foothills of the Gunga Mountains," Amat said. "Only the medicine men are allowed to go there. They believe it is a very powerful place. It's also dangerous. My people are very superstitious. The Christians have tried for years to convert us but our beliefs are strong. This is one of the oldest tribes in all of Sudan and none will venture into the mountains."

"Can we go there?" Alexander asked, trying to hide his excitement. Over the past month, he had learned that the tribe did not respond to enthusiasm because they were worn down from the continuous civil war that had been waged for the past fifty years. They seldom ventured from the village after years of relief organizations dropping food and supplies from the sky. They had no ambition to look further than their own village. The relief workers tried to teach them irrigation and crop rotation, and often their reply would be, "Why work when food falls from the sky?"

Amat translated. He then translated the medicine man's reply for Alexander. "You can go there, but you might not come back."

"What does he mean?" Alexander asked, noticing that the medicine man was still talking. Amat motioned for Alexander to be quiet. "He's talking about the kula. He says only the oldest of my people have seen it. Not good to eat, doesn't bother crops, so we don't think about it. Thought they were gone. Extinct." The medicine man shook his head.

"Do you know where the word is from?"

The medicine man shook his head again.

"Is it poisonous?" Alexander asked.

"Harmless."

Alexander thanked him, took the jar back, and followed Amat back to his tent.

"I've never heard of it," Amat said. "In all my studies."

"I don't understand. I've categorized almost every word, and no one's ever mentioned this kula," Alexander said.

"Our medicine man has seen many things. He just didn't know how to tell you before because he needed to see the bug," Amat said.

"Maybe I haven't been asking the right questions. We need to talk to more villagers, and we'll have to take this beetle back to some of the other villages." Alexander's fingers tapped the Mason jar.

"We're a day from the next village and it's too late for us to start today. Then we must meet with the plane that is scheduled to pick us up," Amat said.

"Can we change the plane?"

"No, my friend, unless you have a satellite phone. We have no way to get in touch with the pilot. The nearest transmitter is at least a day's walk from here. The plane would arrive before the pilot got the message."

Alexander threw his hands up in frustration. His semester-long grant did not cover the cost of a satellite phone for this excursion. Sudan was a difficult place, especially with its lack of modern conveniences like phones or plumbing. It was like stepping back in time a hundred years, and it was hard for an American to accept. "I guess we'll just head out to the next village in the morning and then to the valley."

"All right, my friend. Until then." Amat went into his tent. Alexander walked over to his tent to record his findings in his journal. He brought a lawn chair outside the tent to write about the day's events. He watched the lizards soaking up the late afternoon sun.

The next morning, Alexander followed Amat's path through the tall elephant grass. Amat was carrying a primitive machete to scare away the snakes. Luckily it was the dry season, and most of the snakes were away in search of cool, wet places. They passed the work site where the local relief agency was building a health center. Once completed, the center would have to service 100,000 villagers. It would be the only one in southern Sudan, a vast territory.

They exchanged greetings with a few of the workers. Amat pointed out a few more beetles as they passed the deep trenches of the construction site. They passed nurses from Doctors Without Borders tending to a local who was suffering from a snakebite. The local's arm was swollen and turning black. Alexander turned away.

"If people ask where we are going, don't mention the Valley of the Voices," Amat said as they walked. "They would warn us away."

"I understand. But you can't tell me that no one has ever mapped it or explored it," Alexander said.

"I've heard of a couple geologists from oil companies going there a few years ago, but they never came back, or that's what I heard," Amat said.

It was hard for Alexander to conceive that there was a spot on earth where few people had ever trod. This vast wasteland called Africa was an enigma to him. As they walked through the tall grass, the sun beat down upon them. It was nine in the morning and it was already at least ninety degrees. Alexander took off his Chicago Cubs baseball hat and wiped the sweat from his brow. "Let's stop here for a minute," Amat said.

Alexander opened his pack, drank from his water bottle, and then pulled out two protein bars. He handed one to Amat and sat down in the grass, looking for snakes first. Instead, he saw a black combat boot and jumped back. He looked up and saw two South Sudan militia wearing green camo, holding AK-47s that were pointing at his head.

Both Alexander and Amat raised their hands. "I am from the University of Nairobi," Amat said slowly. "We are here on a research mission."

"Papers?" one soldier said in English. "We must see your papers."

Alexander reached slowly into his pack and pulled out his yellow travel pass, which had been issued in Nairobi. The older soldier walked over to Amat, walked around him staring, and then smiled slowly. Amat nodded in recognition.

The soldier put down his gun as his smile grew larger, displaying large, yellowed teeth. "Captain, it's been so long. I did not recognize you. Forgive me."

"Samir, it's good to see you, my old friend." Amat stood up and shook his hand.

Alexander watched as the two exchanged greetings, not sure what to make of it. "Samir, this is my good friend and colleague, Mr. Alexander."

Samir smiled and shook Alexander's hand. He turned to his fellow soldier. "Put your weapon down. These are friends."

"Tell me, Samir, what are you doing so far out here?" Amat asked.

Samir shook his head. "It is very bad. Young girls were taken from a village not too far from here last night. We're looking for the girls. They're only thirteen."

"This is bad news," Amat said. "Do you know who took them?"

"We think the LRAs got them and are headed to Khartoum. We need to track them before they get there, otherwise the girls are lost," Samir said. "I knew you had retired and were teaching. Why are you in this nowhere?"

"I am a guide for my colleague, Mr. Alexander. I am showing him the history of our peoples. We're headed to the next village to talk to the elders. Mr. Alexander is from university in America and is interested in our languages."

"Very good." Samir nodded, pausing for a minute. "We can take you. Our vehicle is over the hill."

The four men climbed up the hill and got in the army green Jeep. They bounced along on the uneven road. Alexander felt the jolting settle through his uneasy stomach. He held back the acid rising up his throat.

Alexander had waited to ask Amat as he did not want to interrupt the soldiers. "Amat, what is the LRA?"

"It's the Lord's Resistance Army. They are very bad. They claim to be Christians, but they come and steal our children, forcing them to be soldiers or selling them into slavery," Amat said. "The warlord has been indicted for war crimes. There was a very brutal war against the Ugandan government. It went on for many years, and then they fled into the jungles of my country."

Alexander shuddered. It was hard for him to grasp the savagery of this primitive country.

"It's very dangerous for us on both sides of the Nile," Amat said. "We must be careful whom we speak with and what we say. These men are friends. We will be safe with them."

The rising sound of excited children's voices reached Alexander, signaling that they were closer to the village. Each time it started the same way: he would first hear the shouting and then the rustling of the brush as the barefoot children came out running, circling around them.

The vehicle stopped in the center of the village, which was surrounded by a circle of mud huts with thatched roofs. "We will let you out here," Samir said as the car came to a screeching stop.

Alexander and Amat got out of the car. *"D'jaret,"* Amat said. "Good luck finding the girls."

They watched the Jeep drive off at a fast pace, bouncing along the makeshift dirt trail that served as a road. Amat shook his head sadly. "This is getting worse. So many young girls are taken either for the slave trade or killed by the northern Sudanese. Most of them because they are Christians."

Alexander felt the gold cross that hung on the chain around his neck underneath his t-shirt. His mother had given him the family heirloom when he took his first communion. Other than the fact it had belonged her, it bore no significance to him. He didn't believe in the magic that it symbolized. Now it brought him comfort in this forsaken place, reminding him of her gentle touch.

1400 S. Lake Shore Drive, Chicago

Chicago's famed Field Museum is one of the world's greatest natural history museums. It had been conceived during the World's Columbian Exposition in 1893 and moved to its present lakefront home in 1921. From the Dead Sea Scrolls to a complete reconstructed T-Rex named Sue, there was no finer warehouse of historical artifacts. After starting at the museum as a volunteer while in high school, John Lloyd had worked his way up to chief curator by the time he was thirty-five. He didn't look the part with his long salt-and-pepper hair tied in a ponytail.

Tall, pale, and doughy, it was evident that he spent most of his days sitting at a computer, guzzling coffee and Krispy Kreme donuts. He loved all things dead. His brilliant imagination allowed him to experience ancient civilizations as though he were sitting in H.G. Wells's time machine, watching time elapse in front of him—except Wells's machine went into the future and Lloyd's machine went into the past.

Lloyd wiped the glazed sugar from his lips and took one last gulp of his coffee. It was cold by now, but he needed the caffeine. He put on his white cotton gloves and picked up the leather-bound journal of Howard Carter, discoverer of King Tut's tomb.

He gently ran his finger over the drawings of hieroglyphics within the journal, stone rubbings that Carter had done after opening the tomb. The fluorescent lights in his crowded, dinghy office flickered. His computer flashed off. Lloyd reached behind the twenty-seven-inch iMac to restart it. The screen flickered, and a frowning Mac face appeared.

"Shit, it was just working," Lloyd said. He tried doing a hard recovery only to get the same result. "This thing is fried. First time this has happened to me with a Mac." Lloyd had no problem talking to himself. He spent so much time alone that he had started answering himself back.

Lloyd gently closed Carter's journal and placed it back in its glass case for safekeeping. Grabbing his ID badge from the cluttered desk, he walked out into the narrow hallway. He was surrounded by silence; it was nighttime and the museum had been closed for hours. There weren't many people around at this time of night. In fact, there was only the security guard. He walked outside to enjoy a cigarette in the cool spring air. The museum bordered Lake Michigan. Lloyd stood on the limestone steps, feeling the wind rising off the lake. He zipped his Columbia jacket to shield himself from the wind rising off the lake. That's when he heard the sirens in the distance.

Sudan

The children called out to Amat, who always had a smile and kind words for them. They gathered around Amat like he was the Pied Piper.

Then they turned to stare at Alexander with curious eyes, crowding around him. The Africans had no sense of personal space, something that made Alexander uncomfortable. The children held out their hands in greeting. Alexander would shake them per the local custom, yet he was unable to hold back a shudder at the grime. Disease was a very real factor here due to unsanitary conditions and the lack of clean water.

That didn't bother Amat. He laughed off Alexander's concerns with the same shrug he gave when Alexander pulled out his never-ending supply of waterless antibiotic soap. "The dirt gets under your skin, my friend. You will not feel completely clean again until you return to Nairobi," Amat would joke. Alexander didn't even know if he would feel clean in Nairobi, which seemed dusty and overcrowded to him.

He watched Amat shift his heaving duffle bag. He had declined to tell Alexander what was in it. Amat guarded it like it was a bag of gold. It was as heavy as gold, and he would lug it around, never showing any sign of aching muscles.

As Amat chatted with one bright-eyed boy, Alexander swatted at the flies that were everywhere. He didn't understand how the people let the flies perch on their faces, their ragged clothes, their bodies. He couldn't ignore the buzzing and crawling on his skin and was constantly waving them off.

With a few quick words and a wave of his hand, Amat sent the children running toward a large *tukol*. He turned to Alexander. "We will stop at the school, my friend," Amat said, leading the way in the children's direction.

A young man who was slightly cleaner and wearing freshly washed clothes came out of the building. The school had been built on the outskirts of Odella proper; it was in the suburbs of the larger village. He smiled and waved at Amat, who walked over to him.

Alexander listened as the two Africans exchanged words. He couldn't understand all of their conversation. Each village had their own unique dialect, sometimes a completely different language. Even a student of languages as brilliant as Alexander had a hard time grasping the three hundred different lexicons of the southern Sudanese.

Amat finally switched to English. "Alexander, my friend, meet Peter. He is the teacher here," Amat said.

"D'jaret," Alexander said. It meant hello, goodbye, and friendship. He held out his hand to shake hands with the young teacher.

"Peter has been working with the children. He has asked us to stop and give a lesson," Amat said, following Peter into the classroom. Alexander followed the two tall Africans to the front of the classroom. The children were crowded on the dirt floor. It was dark in the school and Alexander strained to make out shapes other than the whites of the children's eyes.

"I'm going to introduce you to the children. First in English and then in Ogoni," Amat said. "Children." He pointed at Alexander. "This is Alexander. He is from America." He turned back to Alexander. "Please say something to the children. I will translate."

"Children, I am here visiting your country to study your people. I will take your story back to my country." As Alexander spoke, Amat translated. He finished and took a step back.

Peter stepped forward and clapped his hands. "Class, let's show our welcome to our guest." One child beat a drum. And then all the children sang. It took a few moments before Alexander realized they were singing "welcome to our school" in halting, stilted English. Tears welled in his eyes as he looked around the room and saw the bright, hopeful faces. These children had no desks, no books, no pencils, no chalkboards. The list could go on and on. He thought of his own students back in Chicago and the complaints he would hear about the lack of Wi-Fi in the classroom or the horrible food in the cafeteria. They were the lucky ones; many of these children in Africa would not even have food tonight. His time in Africa had made him realize the meaning of the word "privileged."

The children finished their song. Wiping his face, Alexander smiled and said, "Thank you." Bending his head, he walked toward the open doorway. "Excuse me." He stepped out into the bright sunlight to collect himself. He came back inside just as Amat was opening up his duffle bag.

"Now children, I have brought you gifts from the church in Nairobi." Amat pulled out exercise books. "These books will help you learn, and I have one for each child in the village. We also have writing instruments for you."

Alexander watched as Peter and Amat passed out the books and pencils. The children clasped the books carefully. A girl turned the pages, running her fingers along the words. One boy clutched the book to his chest. Alexander looked away in embarrassment, thinking how much paper was wasted each week on the celebrity tabloids and his own boxed-up collection of books in the basement of his Chicago home.

Amat conducted a brief reading lesson in both English and the native tribal language. Alexander watched as Amat had the children read from their primary readers. Following the class, Alexander walked outside with the teacher and Amat. "We will go into the village, my friend, and bring your curious bug to the chief," Amat said.

"Wait. This is my star pupil," Peter said, bringing a boy about ten years old over to Alexander and Amat.

"Hello, Mesabo," Amat said to the boy. Alexander recognized him as the boy Amat had talked to when they first arrived in the village.

"Hello," the boy replied, looking down at the ground. His feet were bare and dusty. Dirt clung to any skin not covered by a pair of castoff shorts and a San Francisco Giants t-shirt, donations from a relief organization.

"Mesabo would like to talk to you, Mr. Alexander," Peter said, putting his hand on the boy's shoulder. "Do you have a few minutes?"

"Certainly. Please follow me." Alexander led the way underneath a shaded rain tree. He and the boy sat down across from each other. A group of children gathered around and watched curiously.

"I am very interested in your country," the boy said in halting English.

"How do you speak such good English?" Alexander asked, swatting away a fly.

"Mr. Peter has been teaching me after school. My dream is to be well-learned like you and Mr. Amat."

"That's very good. How can I help you?"

"You can go to your America and tell them about us. About how we cannot learn because we have no books, no teachers, and no tools. We need tools. We want to learn." The boy's eyes burned with a passion that had been missing from Alexander's own classroom for years.

"I will do that," Alexander promised. "I will go back and tell my people about you and your school."

"This is good. The more people that know or that come see us, the more people will know about our troubles. I want to follow Mr. Amat and go to school to teach so I can come back here like Mr. Peter."

"That's great." Alexander was impressed by the boy's earnestness and promised to help him with his dream.

"I want to go see your America and learn there so I can come back here and teach."

"Come see me when you are ready to come to America. I will help you," Alexander said.

"How far do I walk?" The boy asked.

Alexander smiled. "It's many miles across great water."

"Oh, the river," the boy said in broken English.

"It's further than that. First you have to cross the Nile then pass another great body of water."

The boy pondered. He couldn't conceive of any land that was too far to walk to. The vastness of the world was a mystery to him. Explaining it was impossible without the help of a book or globe to demonstrate.

Alexander reached around his neck and removed a gold chain. Attached to the chain was a silver compass. "When I was your age, a great man gave this to me to remind me I am never too far from home," Alexander said, holding the compass in his hand, balancing it in his fingers. He handed it to Mesabo.

Mesabo held the shiny compass in his palm. He stared at it.

"This will help you find me when you are ready to come to America. When you are ready, follow the 'w' pointing west." Standing up, Alexander demonstrated on the compass. The boy stood up, staring over Alexander's shoulder. "When you reach America, I'll be there for you. When you need my help, you will find me at the end of this 'w.'"

"W," Mesabo repeated. "Thank you." Mesabo put the compass around his neck. In return, he took off his necklace of native beads and handed it to Alexander.

"Thank you." Alexander took the necklace, studied it and then placed it around his neck. Each tribe had its own colors; this one was brown and red. He had found the southern Sudanese a very generous people, continuously offering him gifts from their meager possessions. To not accept the gift would be an insult. He felt bad accepting these treasures from people who had nothing, but their pride meant more than the possessions.

Alexander stood up and looked for Amat, who was sitting nearby on an antelope skin circled by a group of men. He turned to walk over to them. Mesabo stood where Alexander left him, staring at the compass. He ran his finger along the "w."

"My friend, we must go to the village. The medicine man is waiting." Amat stood up and waved as Alexander came up to him. "It is not far."

Alexander followed Amat along the worn path. Many children and villagers followed them. The women and young girls balanced heavy baskets filled with water on their heads. By the time they reached Odella, the village, it was late afternoon. Alexander's feet ached in his heavy hiking boots, his clothes clung to him dampened with sweat, and his water bottle was nearly empty. His shoulder was sore from carrying his heavy backpack. He tossed back a couple of salt tablets and marveled at Amat's cool exterior. The heat did not seem to affect Amat at all. They were greeted by children and tribespeople who were proudly wearing wool clothes that had been donated by church ladies in North America. Alexander would have gone naked before donning the itchy wool.

Amat sent one of the village children to notify the elder that the visitor had arrived. The elder came out of his *tukol* followed by his council. They passed around a ceremonial pipe. Alexander held himself back during this ceremonial meeting. He wished they would get to the point, but these people made a ceremony out of his visit. In every village it had been the same. There was no way past the rituals. After an hour and a half of smoking and drinking, Alexander was finally able to remove the jar from his backpack. Upon seeing it, all the elders mumbled among themselves. Alexander couldn't understand any words except for the occasional "kula." He handed it to the medicine man, who studied it. The medicine man laughed and said something to Amat.

"He says you've captured a rain beetle. He wants to know where you got it," Amat translated.

"In the Agunwi village," Alexander said.

The medicine man nodded and said something to Amat, who looked at Alexander and translated. "The trenches are bringing them up."

"Kuot, come here." The medicine man waved his arm and called out to a boy who looked around eight years old. He was wearing a pair of tattered shorts and a Nike t-shirt. The boy looked at the bug and laughed with his grandfather. He said something.

"The boy says the bug looks like the picture in the cave," Amat said.

"Cave? What cave?" Alexander asked, rolling up to his knees in his enthusiasm.

Amat shared his enthusiasm, filled with the same curiosity.

"Slow down." Amat motioned for Alexander to sit again. He translated something. The boy and his grandfather exchanged a few words. The medicine man then turned and said something to Amat. "He says his grandson will lead us there. He has traveled there before with the medicine man." Amat continued, "Because the boy has the blood of medicine men, he alone can travel to the Valley of the Voices with us."

It was two miles from Odella to the mountain pass. The sides of the path were surrounded by cliffs and overhangs a thousand feet high, with little vegetation. The pass was a mile-long walk and an easy trek during the dry season, except for the need to avoid the occasional puff adder. The boy walked at a fast pace with no apparent fear of snakes. Alexander walked carefully with each step; the thought of the slithery creatures was making him uneasy. During his travels throughout sub-Saharan Africa, he had seen puff adders, vipers, cobras, and green tree snakes. He had watched a relief doctor care for a villager who had been bitten while she was sleeping. Her arm swelled from the toxins and paralysis quickly set in. By morning, she was dead. There were so many types of snakes. They were in the ground, in the trees, in the water. Alexander's skin crawled.

He glanced down at his dust-covered boots. The dark rich soil resembled powdered chocolate pudding. His eyes darted back and forth along the ground, waiting for a flash of movement. Alexander understood why no one wanted to make this journey in the rainy season, as that was when the most snake bites occurred. A couple of days of rain and it would be a sea of mud.

At the end of the pass, there was a clearing of dry, brown grass. The valley was surrounded on all sides by mountains, the tallest of which was three thousand feet.

Amat pointed. "That's where we're going. The east ridge."

As Alexander watched Amat enter the valley, he thought back to the first time he had met him.

***

Alexander had landed in Nairobi three months ago. Although he was a seasoned traveler who grew up in a military family, it still hadn't prepared him for the wild African landscape and customs, some of which dated back thousands of years. He had left London in the evening and slept fitfully most of the way, crammed into economy class. They had arrived in Nairobi in the morning. Planes couldn't land at night due to the altitude.

He followed his fellow passengers out of the plane and to the customs area. His backpack, which he had filled with PowerBars, Gatorade, and freeze-dried food, felt heavy on his shoulders. He set it down to fill out the one-page transit form and to ease his aching shoulders. When it was finally his turn, he walked up to the clerk, passport in hand. The attendant scanned his passport and stared him in the face.

"Reason for travel?" he asked with a stern expression.

"Transit," came Alexander's reply. Amat, his correspondent at the University of Nairobi, had instructed him on what to say. "I will only be here three days until I travel to Sudan."

"Thirty dollars," the man replied, stamping his passport and pocketing the money.

He scribbled out a receipt, which Alexander shoved in his pocket. He followed the path to baggage claim, where he waited by the carousel. As he waited, he looked around for Amat. The two had been corresponding via email after meeting in an academic chat room. As their plans had developed, they had switched to Skype, so Alexander felt confident he would recognize Amat. While Alexander's interests lay in cataloguing the many tribal languages of Sudan, Amat's were in studying the rich history of his people. After having grown up in the Sudan, Amat, with the help of Christian missionaries, had been educated in Nairobi and was now a professor of history at the University of Nairobi. He would also be serving as Alexander's guide on this trip.

Alexander grabbed his duffle bag off the carousel just as he spotted what he thought was a familiar face. A tall, lean African man wearing a well-fitting black suit and black-framed glasses walked toward him, his hand extended. "Alexander, my friend," he said in accented English. Alexander felt that he would have recognized him anywhere.

"Amat," Alexander replied, shaking his hand. "It's good to meet you in person."

Alexander felt dirty in his travel-worn jeans and t-shirt standing next to the neatly clad Amat. He had been in the air for more than twenty-four hours with no time between flights to freshen up.

"Are these your bags?" Amat asked, pointing at the two duffle bags, laptop case, and backpack at Alexander's feet.

Alexander nodded.

"Let's go then. I have a car outside." Amat picked up both duffle bags and headed toward the sliding glass doors.

Alexander grabbed his laptop and backpack and followed him out. Immediately he was hit with the humid air. It clung to his skin, making sweat beads appear on his brow. He followed Amat to a white Renault and listened to the babble of voices that surrounded him outside the crowded airport. Mixed with English were phrases of what Alexander assumed to be Swahili and French, among others.

He settled into the passenger seat of the car. Amat started the engine and took off down the highway, avoiding the bumps and potholes in the street with the skill of a racecar driver. Alexander watched the scene out the window, disbelieving his eyes. The images resembled those he had only seen on the Travel Channel or in *National Geographic*. People displayed their wares in shabbily constructed corner stalls crafted from leftover pieces of corrugated aluminum and twigs. Women were walking to and from the city balancing baskets on their heads. Scantily clad shoeless children were leading skinny cattle to the marketplace. Dust was everywhere—on the car, on the people, filling the air.

They hit a bump and Alexander's head hit the roof. "I'm sorry, my friend," Amat said. "The Nairobi government is so corrupt, they cannot determine whose responsibility it is to fix the roads. Instead they do nothing."

When they reached the center of Nairobi, they experienced a traffic jam like nothing Alexander had seen in Chicago. Cars were parked everywhere, even in the middle of the streets. Amat swerved his way around them, following the path of crowded minibuses and other drivers ahead of him. People walked across the street with no regard for traffic even as cars sped by. Amat explained that this was simply the way people drove.

They entered a neighborhood that appeared to be middle class. The homes were surrounded by wooden gates and each had a large wooden barricade leading up to its drive. Amat pulled into one of these drives and honked. A young girl appeared on the other side, sliding the gate open. Amat pulled the car in and up a steep driveway. The girl hurriedly closed the gate and locked it.

"Here we are, my friend. I thought you might want to freshen up before we go meet with the Sudanese authorities in Nairobi," Amat said, leading the way into the house.

Alexander looked around. The house was built along European lines, with a large hallway carved out in mahogany and wood parquet flooring. One side of the hallway opened into a formal living room with a fireplace, and the other opened into a formal dining room. Alexander followed Amat down the hall. The African opened a door to a small bedroom decorated in dark wood.

"This is where you will stay until we leave for Sudan. I hope it is satisfactory," Amat said. He placed the duffle bags on a bench at the foot of the bed.

"It will be perfect. Thank you for letting me stay in your home," Alexander replied. He put his laptop bag onto the bed.

"Why don't you freshen yourself and rest? I'll have Magda call you when dinner is ready," Amat said.

"Thank you. That sounds great," Alexander replied.

"The restroom is right next door. Call if you need anything." Amat walked out, closing the door behind him.

Alexander was exhausted from his two long plane rides; he sat on the edge of the bed looking around the room. He had a strange sensation of déjà vu. He strained to keep his eyes open but couldn't fight off the fatigue. He lay down on the bed and slept well except for a disturbing dream about a cave.

"Mr. Alexander, Mr. Alexander," Magda called through the door, lightly tapping. Her soft rhythmic voice woke Alexander. He felt rested and refreshed. And hungry. Somehow airline food was never enough, and this would be his last good meal before he had to start on his stash of granola, PowerBars, and almonds.

When he walked into the dining room, Amat was sitting at the head of a large teak table. "My friend, please join me." Amat stood as Alexander took a seat to his right.

They exchanged pleasantries and collegial stories over the meal of rice, sausage, cassava, and fried bananas. After dinner, they adjourned to Amat's study for cigars. The walls of the study were Koa wood and decorated with tribal masks and native fertility dolls. Alexander looked at a picture on the mantle. It showed a beautiful young woman with three boys and a girl. "You have a beautiful family," Alexander said, picking it up to look closer at it.

Amat placed the picture neatly back on the mantle and ran a loving finger over it. He smiled. "Thank you. There have been many terrible losses in the war."

"I'm sorry." Alexander stared at the floor.

"This is a tribal mask of the Agunwi tribe," Amat said, pointing to one of the masks on the wall. "It signifies the tribe's motto of peace under courage. See the bird." Amat talked about the mask and its symbols. "As you know, my friend, northern Sudan has been waging its war over southern Sudan for the past fifty years. They've been holding my people hostage. They've bombed the schools, the hospitals, and the villages. My people go without much. Northern Sudan won't let food reach my people. They are starving. Babies are dying because they don't have access to the simplest of vaccines. All in the name of religion. We go tomorrow to the rebel army headquarters here to ask their permission for us to travel in southern Sudan. We need a pass from them to get into the country. But that is tomorrow."

Amat walked over to the folding card table in the corner of the room. "Here, look, my friend, this is our route." Alexander followed him to the table. Covering the table was a map of Sudan. The northern boundary was split from the southern by the curving Nile.

"Here is where we will enter Sudan." Amat drew a line on the map with his finger. "We will go to these villages. Finally we will end up here. The government has permitted a relief organization to come in to work with the people. We will end up at their camp because there is a landing strip there. That's where our pilot will drop us off and pick us up. The conditions can be very treacherous. Are you ready, my friend?" Amat looked at Alexander.

"As ready as I can be. I've read everything I can find about your people, but I couldn't find as much as I had hoped." Alexander sat down into a red leather armchair.

"That's because our language is spoken, not written. There are so many different tribes and so many different variations in our languages. Travel is difficult. There are no roads, only brush. It can take days to get to the next village. These are a remote people." Amat poured two glasses of brandy from a carafe, handed one to Alexander, and sat down across from him.

"I want to look for the origin of the language," Alexander took a sip.

"You shall, my friend, you shall."

"Is it safe? What about snakes?" Alexander asked.

Amat laughed. "Don't worry about snakes. It is the dry season. They are away in dark, damp places."

This reminded Alexander of his dream about the cave.

Current Day, Sudan

"The cave?" Alexander said out loud, stirring from his thoughts.

"Did you say something?" Amat turned around and asked him.

"Nothing." Alexander shook his head. "How much further to the cave?"

"It's just right over that ridge." Amat pointed as they climbed up the mountain. During the long hike to the cave, which happened to be on the side of what Alexander decided must be the largest mountain in Africa, the boy relayed the history of the cave. Alexander relied on Amat to translate. Sweat poured off Alexander's brow as he followed Amat and the boy, who were about ten feet in front of him. Alexander popped a few more salt tablets. His hiking boots felt like they had been encased in concrete, and his calves ached. In comparison, Amat in his hiking boots and the boy in his bare feet were walking faster than him.

Alexander felt a cool breeze as he drew near the cave's entrance. He smelled the dampness and mold. The boy and Amat were sitting on a rock outside the cave. Alexander bent over for a moment trying to catch his breath. The boy pointed inside the cave. "He says the drawings are in there," Amat translated.

Alexander pulled out his heavy-duty flashlight and turned it on. The boy stared in amazement. Alexander stepped lightly inside the cave, waiting for a hissing sound. It was pitch dark inside. He could hear the sound of running water from somewhere deep inside. The boy led them down several winding passages until they reached the level of the drawings. What Alexander saw knocked the breath out of him. He wished his mom were here to see it. It appeared to be some kind of hieroglyphics—symbols he'd never seen before. None of it made any sense, but somehow it all made sense. The pictures were similar to Egyptian hieroglyphics and had writing that resembled Aramaic.

And right in the middle was a picture of the beetle. Alexander pulled out his iPhone and took pictures. As the flash went off, bats swirled around his head, shrieking at the explosion of light. After he took his last picture, he reached for the flashlight, which he had placed in a crevice. "SSSS" he heard, just as his hand reached there. Alexander froze.

"Be still," Amat's voice came from behind him. "It's a spitting cobra. If angered, it will spit venom into your eyes and you will die. Turn your face."

"What do you mean turn my face?" Alexander whispered, slowly following the instructions.

With one swift move, Amat chopped the snake's head off with his machete. The snake continued to hiss as it fell to the ground, the tail piece stretching at least six feet long. Alexander jumped back out of its way.

"Thank you."

"No problem, my friend."

Alexander's mind returned back to his findings. "Ask him—where did these drawings come from?"

Amat asked. The boy shook his head. "Do you know who did this?" Amat asked for Alexander. The boy shook his head again.

"This is big—really big. I've never seen anything resembling these drawings."

Reaching around Alexander, Amat took out his knife and carved out a piece of the rock. "For testing when we return home," Amat said to Alexander. "The plane is coming tomorrow."

"I need more time." Alexander studied the drawings.

"If you don't leave now, you will be stuck in Sudan for more than three months."

"That's okay." Alexander waved the matter away, not concerned with the consequences. "I need to find out what this is."

"But it will be the rainy season," Amat reminded him.

The rainy season. The villagers had told him stories about the snakes that were everywhere during the rainy season and the mud that clung to your boots until you were inches taller. He shone his flashlight on the floor and saw the two pieces of the spitting cobra. He shuddered. "I'll leave tomorrow."

"That's what I thought. Good decision." Amat nodded.

"I need to be home anyway for the beginning of the spring semester." Alexander hit the light button on his phone to confirm how much time he had left. He'd have to make it to Loki and back to Nairobi to catch his return flight. He tapped his phone. "That's odd," he mused out loud. Time was running backwards. He tapped it several times but nothing changed. "I must have hit it on a rock." He dismissed it with a shrug.

***

The next morning, Alexander stepped out of his mud hut and stretched. It was his last morning here. At some point, the plane would show up to bring him back to the life he had left behind. The makeshift landing strip outside the relief center was just big enough for the single-engine Cessna. This would be the last flight to Loki before the start of the rainy season. The pilot, a retired Swedish Air Force captain named Stan Hillstrom, had flown the relief route for the past few years, bringing supplies to the workers.

Three months ago, Stan had flown Alexander and Amat from Loki to southern Sudan. Now, Alexander saw Amat waving to him from the airstrip.

"He's here," Amat called. Alexander watched the tall Swede unloading supplies from the tail of the plane, which was covered by the dust that seemed to surround all of southern Sudan.

"Stan," Alexander yelled, walking towards him.

Stan turned around with a smile of recognition on his face and shook Alexander's hand. "Give me a hand unloading this so we can head back to Loki before dark," Stan said in heavily accented English.

Alexander grabbed wooden crates marked World Relief and set them down in the back of the waiting Land Rover.

"That's it," Stan said, closing the Cessna's tail. "Let's head back." He climbed up into the pilot's seat.

Climbing into the plane, Alexander started to head to the back seat. "No, my friend, you sit in the copilot's seat; it'll give you a better view," Amat said, fastening his seat belt from where he sat in back.

Stan started the plane's engine. The takeoff was rough, but they cleared the trees at the end of the run heading out over the dingy brown savanna. Alexander was caught up in the vastness of the landscape. The hum of the engine was lulling him to sleep. He was exhausted after all the excitement of the past few weeks. He didn't realize how tired he was. He had lost twenty pounds and his jeans hung loosely off his narrow frame. His eyes began to droop closed.

That's when the first bullet blasted through the hull of the plane and ricocheted past his head. Alexander's eyes flew open and he sat upright, clutching the armrests of the co-pilot's chair. "Hang on," Stan shouted, his accent growing thicker, and as his years of military training kicked in, so did his adrenaline.

The second bullet grazed Amat's leg as Stan took the plane to a hard left and then into a barrel roll. Alexander felt his stomach turn inside out. He turned around to see Amat holding his leg, blood dripping down.

"Amat, you've been shot. What's going on? Who's shooting at us?"

"It's the LRA," Stan shouted. "They've been shooting at relief planes. I didn't know they were on this side of the Nile, sums of bitches." Stan had flown much more dangerous sorties than this, but it pissed him off that he wasn't allowed to carry weapons on relief missions. He reached into the overhead compartment to pull out an emergency kit and handed it to Amat.

"It just grazed me," Amat said, opening the kit and wrapping his leg with gauze.

"Jesus," Alexander said. "The Lord's Resistance Army. That's the one your soldier friend, Samir, was telling us about?"

Amat just nodded his head.

Stan reached under his seat, pulling out a .45. He opened the window and wove his arm around the frame.

"Sum of bitches." He shot haphazardly. The sounds of the AK-47s disappeared behind them as they flew away from the scattered ground troops.

"No damage to the plane. We'll be fine," Stan said as they entered Kenyan airspace and touched down on the small airstrip at Loki. Their Cessna was surrounded by other planes, bearing logos ranging from World Relief to Doctors Without Borders. As they exited the plane, Stan exchanged greetings with other pilots, sharing their experience loudly.

Lokichoggio, Kenya

Alexander sat on a tall stool in the cantina. The building was fashioned out of tin and had a green corrugated tin roof. The round bar was made out of plains grass and teak wood. A small stage was carved out of one side across from the bar. The tin roof cast a dark glow throughout the bar. Alexander's eyes had taken minutes to adjust to the dark after being out in the searing sun. The bar smelled of sweat, spilt beer, and piss. This was where the relief workers came to rest after spending long weeks in the field.

"Here you go for your baptism by fire," Stan said, walking up to him carrying three shot glasses and a bottle. He handed one glass to Alexander and said "Ska." They clanked the glasses together and Stan downed his in one gulp.

Alexander downed his too, feeling it burn down his throat until the warmth hit his stomach. "What was that?"

"Whiskey," Stan said, refilling their shot glasses. "We were lucky today. My friend, Thor, wasn't."

Walking up to the table, Amat said, "Let me have one of those." He pointed to the third shot glass. Amat's leg was still bandaged in white gauze and he was walking with a slight limp.

Stan filled the glass so it overflowed and the whiskey dripped over the sides. Amat downed it and sat on the empty chair next to Alexander.

"Are you okay?" Alexander asked.

"It's nothing. Just a scratch."

"Why was the LRA shooting at us? World Relief is trying to help feed their people." Alexander asked, refilling his glass.

"The warlords are just as corrupt as our politicians. In the north, we have the Muslims trying to kill us. And in the south we have the Christian warlords trying to control us. They feel that any outside help threatens their power," Amat explained.

"Enough politics." Stan refilled their three shot glasses. "Your flight to Nairobi leaves early in the morning; until then, let's get drunk."

As Stan filled Alexander's glass, Alexander noticed a large, colorful tattoo on his forearm and pointed at it. "Valkyrie. That's an interesting story."

"I got that in Libya when we were called in to support the no-fly zone. I was shot down by a surface-to-air missile, tortured by al Qaeda. After I escaped, I swore I would never be taken prisoner again. Like my Viking forefathers, I want to die on the battlefield and have the Valkyries fly me to Valhalla and drink in the great hall. Fuck these LRA." Stan downed his glass and slammed it down on the table. The drinks poured throughout the night as other pilots joined them to hear Stan share stories about his wild fighting days.

Like his last night in the Agunwi village, Alexander drank until he nearly passed out. He stumbled to the barracks with Amat and settled onto the military cot. As he drifted off, he dreamed of dark angels flying over a scorched earth.

Glasgow, Scotland

Rebekah looked around the lecture room following her presentation. She encountered some blank stares but also found some students nodding with interest and understanding. She checked her watch. Her lecture had run short; there were still a few minutes left. "Does anyone have any questions?"

"I get the concept of chaotic math, but how is it applied to the real world? Like why should we care?" a young female student asked.

Rebekah thought for a moment. "It's being used now to explain everything from time and space to God. Chaotic math is more than just a bunch of formulas. It's a concept—a way of thinking. If used properly, it provides a way to release the restraints of our own limited thinking and opens up a whole new world."

"Explain what you mean by a whole new way of thinking," one student asked, interrupting her.

Rebekah walked over to the podium where her Mac Powerbook was balanced and flicked on an overhead projector. She drew what appeared to be a scribbled line going in many different directions. "The general meaning of chaos implies unpredictability of a path. Chaotic math solves that problem. For instance, as you trace this line out frame by frame, it would be difficult to guess the next move and where the line will end. With chaotic math, the curve, like every other occurrence, can be mapped with a mathematical formula. You can, in fact, predict what the curve will do next in this drawing and what its final shape will be by using the general principles of chaotic math."

She walked back over to her laptop. She drew a crosshair and placed numbers on the horizontal axis, marking the vertical axis 0 and moving to the left with -1, -2, -3 and then going to the right with positive numbers 1, 2, 3. "So what might appear to the naked eye as unfathomably complex is in reality governed by a relatively simple mathematical expression. Notice you can trace where the lines will connect on the horizontal and vertical planes of this diagram. As the lines cross over each other, they touch on points along both axes, negative and positive, at different intervals. As you may have read about Bowen's Theory in which trajectories will move at a predictable speed going toward a closed curve, but further out, these lines go in both directions; they will eventually start moving closer to the interval lines at an even rate until they reach a point where we will be able to predict where they will be able to land."

Looking around the classroom, she saw a number of blank faces staring back at her. She continued, "In other words, there's no difference between this complex path and the path along a straight line. It is simply that a straight line path leads the eye in an obvious way from the start to the end point."

The girl stood up again and asked, "What about variables? You say you can use it to predict abstracts such as God, but how do you adjust for an omnipresent, all-knowing, invisible entity?"

The class laughed. Rebekah grinned. "The essence of chaos in science is just that—a relatively complex behavior that is strictly governed by a mathematical algorithm but nonetheless unpredictable due to sensitivity to initial conditions. Although in principle we can predict how a system will behave to an arbitrary level of precision, in practice we can't find the initial starting point of the system accurately enough to be able to predict in detail what will happen beyond a short period of time. Small mismeasurements eventually add up to a big discrepancy between calculated and observed behavior.

"The sure-fire way to have a system described by an algorithm that exhibits chaotic behavior," Rebekah continued, "is to have it be nonlinear. The importance of studying chaotic behavior lies in the fact that most systems encountered in the real world, including God, are nonlinear to some extent and either exhibit chaotic behavior or can be made to exhibit it. In fact, chaos is observed in so many systems in the real world that some scientists rank the understanding of chaos as being as important as the theories of relativity and quantum mechanics in that its ramifications stretch into every aspect of scientific study.

"As far as God is concerned, he may move in mysterious ways. Those mysterious ways have mathematical formulas, but we haven't found them yet," Rebekah concluded. The class laughed.

A deep, raspy voice with a thick Scottish brogue boomed from the back of the auditorium. "What do you mean when you say that a system is chaotic if it is nonlinear?"

Rebekah smiled in recognition. That voice brought back memories of twilight hikes on the Scottish moors and all-night discussions with harsh words and harsher Scotch. "We are by our nature linear-thinking creatures. We learn to read a book by reading one page after another. When we watch a film, we are watching twenty-four frames per second moving in a beginning-to-end format to form a single picture, or thought, in our heads. This system works great for most of our lives, if we're reading a Harlequin romance or watching Charlton Heston in a chariot race, but to grasp the idea of systems that don't follow this pattern, we must open up our minds. The first step is understanding the bipolar theory of chaotic math."

"What's that?" a student piped up from the front row.

"I'm glad you asked," Rebekah replied. The class laughed. "Bipolar explains the fact that time is always moving in two directions." She walked to the laptop again and drew a circle with a straight line through the center and arrows pointing in a forward and backward direction. "Right now as I speak to you, we are in the here and now represented by this circle. As time passes, we are moving closer to the future." To demonstrate, she drew a circle around the forward arrow. "But at the same time, we're moving farther away from the past which itself is moving farther away from us in this direction." She circled the arrow going backwards. "That is the essence of chaotic math. The past helps predict the future because the past is always affecting the future." She turned off the overhead projector, closed her laptop and glanced at the clock. "Speaking of the future, I see that we are out of time; thank you, students."

"Bravo," the voice from the back boomed once again as the students filed out of the auditorium. Walking up to her was a gray-haired man with a barrel chest and hairy legs unhidden by his traditional Scottish attire. He had a chiseled face that was weatherworn and windblown. The ruddy nose, however, was the result of too-many bottles of Glenfiddich.

"Professor McLean, I'm glad you made it," Rebekah said.

"I wouldn't miss your first lecture for the world. Now that the student has surpassed the teacher, Angus will do, my lass," he said, walking up on the stage.

Rebekah flushed and said, "That will never happen. It is a relief to be finished with that." Rebekah packed her materials and her laptop into her briefcase. "Will you join me for a drink?"

"That's a dangerous invitation to pose to an old Scotsman," he replied.

She laughed as they left the auditorium. They walked past Pierce Hall on the way to The High Road Pub, a journey they had made many times during her undergraduate days. The walk to the pub was the easy one; it was the walk back that took some maneuvering, as she often found herself leading Angus, who was three kilts to the wind. Moderation was not a word in Angus's vocabulary.

"Ach, it's like coming home," Angus said as they walked the street and saw the sign to the pub.

"Angus," came the collective voice of the regulars as the professor opened the door and walked in. Rebekah followed him down the stone steps of what had once been the distillery for the monks who had sold their whiskey and ale to the local townspeople. All the university land had once belonged to a monastery.

Two young college students were playing darts in the far corner of the pub. Angus walked between the player and the dartboard. The younger of the two players said, "Number 20," handing Angus a dart.

With that challenge, Angus swiftly pivoted from his hips and threw the dart, hitting the number 20. This was the start of what would be many a free drink.

Angus turned and bowed to Rebekah. "Your turn." He handed her the dart. "Lass, a bull's-eye will buy you a pint."

The two lads nodded, accepting the challenge. Rebekah took the dart and, without looking, threw it. It landed perfectly in the center of the board. The boys sang, "Fair lassie lay waiting the hills covered green, a maiden of Scotland none fairer I've seen." One of them brought her a pint of the local ale. The whole pub joined in: "Her heart was so pure that the angels would sing, Trula Uont Nokan, we bow to our queen." The whole pub raised their glasses and then bowed towards Rebekah. She raised her glass and curtsied in return. She followed Angus to his favorite corner table. The waitress brought them over a plate of haggis. "So lass, where to from here?" Angus said before finishing off his drink.

"I have received several offers from universities back in the States; I haven't decided on which one to accept." She stared down at the haggis-filled plate Angus put in front of her. "I sure won't miss this pile of sheep crap you call food, but I have grown accustomed to you, you old goat!"

Four years ago, if you would have told Rebekah that she would be sitting in a pub in the University of Glasgow, drinking with the father of chaotic math, she would have laughed in your face; the phrase "old goat" would have earned you a right hook and a bad headache.

When she first arrived, she had been an awestruck math groupie. Angus was the Scottish mathematician version of Elvis and Glasgow was Graceland. Seeing her enthusiasm, Angus had taken her under his wing and became more than a mentor.

He swallowed down a bite of haggis that would have choked a horse and rinsed it down with a second glass of Glenfiddich. "You know, Rebekah, there have been no finer than you. You have the opportunity and the capability to take our work to a new level. The possibilities are limitless. I've nearly finished the preliminary testing on the chaotic correlator program."

"And?" Rebekah leaned closer across the wood table, her eyes wide.

"I think his mysterious ways are becoming less a mystery."

"What have you found?"

Angus pulled his chair next to her, looked around, and spoke in a lower voice. He said, "I fed in pages from every known religious work—the Torah, the Koran, and the Bible, everything from voodoo to Kabbalah. Besides the usual correlations you would imagine you would find, such as a powerful being and references to good and evil, there was one phrase that carried through all of the differences in beliefs."

Rebekah took a drink. "What is it?"

"In the beginning was the word," Angus said, and downed his pint.

30,000 Feet over the Atlantic

Alexander sat on the plane, bound for the States. He had had a twelve-hour layover in London—just enough time to switch airports by shuttle bus. There'd been no time to check his email at Heathrow as he had hoped. Instead he was stuck in this tin can watching the same movies over and over. He flipped through the personal screen on the back of the seat in front of him. He came across an old favorite, *The Quiet Man* starring John Wayne and Maureen O'Hara. He remembered watching it on St. Patrick's Day with his mom. He had missed being in Chicago for the parade and celebration and was glad to be returning. It was now early April, and the rains had begun in Sudan.

He popped a few more Xanax and pulled out his book of crossword puzzles. It was his third book of *New York Times* challenges this trip. Listening to Maureen O'Hara's voice brought back memories of his mother. Leaning back, he closed his eyes.

She had been a poor Irish immigrant who taught herself to read. With a true love for knowledge, she read everything and even taught herself several languages so she could read the masters in their original form. Alexander had received his love of knowledge from her. When he studied languages, he felt close to her. Like she wasn't really gone. Sometimes he felt the fingertips of a ghost smoothing his hair like she used to.

He remembered that Easter morning when she had fixed his hair and let her hand linger there for one moment. Alexander had been wearing a new suit. His mom was wearing a new dress and hat. Hand in hand, they had walked along the city streets on their way to church. At seven, he was glad to have his mom to himself. His dad had been called to Washington to start his new position at the quartermaster's office. He was looking for a house and was going to get settled before Alexander and his mom would join him.

They reached the steps of St. Catherine's Church on the north side of Chicago. Next to Christmas, it was the biggest holiday of the religious year, so his mom wanted to get there early to get a seat. He loved going to church with her. It was more of a magical place than a holy place. Its magic lay in this fantastic puzzle called the Bible. Each page was a piece of a greater picture. He loved hearing the stories. The religious icons and stained glass windows added to the beauty of the experience.

When the priests spoke in Latin, his mom would translate for him. Eventually he picked up enough to understand the gist of what they were saying. Sometimes his thoughts wandered, though. That Easter, he couldn't help sneaking glances at his mom. He always knew she was beautiful with her flaming red hair and big green eyes; however, he thought she was more beautiful than every other mother there. And today, she had taken particular care with her appearance. Not only in honor of Easter, but also in honor of the visiting missionary she had invited over for dinner.

Speaking from the pulpit, the senior priest introduced the young missionary. "Our missionary from Ethiopia, Father Paul, is joining us today. Our prayers have been with him throughout the months. I'd like to have him say a few words about the church's work in bringing the word of God to the many villages in Africa. Father Paul, please tell us about your work."

Father Paul was barely out of seminary. He was lit with the fire for the Lord. Unfortunately, it would be years before Vatican II would free the Catholic Church to match this young hippie's passion. He looked like he'd just come from the jungle with his bushy black hair and untrimmed beard. He was wearing torn jeans with a safari jacket and his priest collar. Even for this most sacred of days, he'd refused to don his vestments. It wasn't a selling technique; he'd been in the bush so long he had a hard time assimilating back into so-called civilized cultures.

"God be with you. I'm Father Paul; as many of you know who write to me, I run a mission and a jungle hospital in the Blue Nile region of Ethiopia." Alexander only half-listened until Father Paul brought out a tribal mask. Then Alexander perked up. This was not the usual pomp and circumstance. This was something new and exciting to a seven-year-old boy. When the service finally ended, Alexander couldn't wait to ask questions and touch the mask.

His mom had to curb his enthusiasm and told him not to bother Father Paul as he stood greeting parishioners as they left the church. "He'll be a guest at our house," she had said. "You can ask him questions later."

Although it was barely a half hour after church ended, it seemed forever to Alexander until Father Paul arrived. He showed up at the door bearing a bottle of wine and native animal statues carved from koa wood for Alexander. When he had talked about Africa, it might as well have been the moon. Both seemed just as far and as exotic a land to a seven-year-old. He hoped to visit both someday.

The three sat down to a traditional Easter feast of ham and sweet potatoes. Throughout dinner, Father Paul talked more of Africa and Alexander's mom talked of Ireland. Father Paul offered to help with the dishes, but was sentenced to the den to light a fire. Alexander helped his mom with the dishes.

"Mom, can I go talk to Father Paul now? Can I go? Can I go?" Alexander asked.

Looking at his eager face, she couldn't say no and sent him off to the den.

"Excuse me, Father Paul, can you tell me more about Africa?" Alexander asked, sitting on the ottoman in front of the fire. He faced the young priest.

Father Paul leaned down from his easy chair to better talk to the boy. "It's a beautiful land. It has deserts and rainforests."

"What about the animals? Did you see lions and elephants and giraffes?"

"I've seen it all in Africa, Alexander. After a while, it just becomes part of the scenery. What really is amazing is the people. Bringing the word to the people and watching them give their hearts to the Lord."

"Tell me about the mask," Alexander asked, brushing off the talk about God.

"It was given to me by the chief of the Waguna tribe. The mask symbolizes peace. It's made from wood and antelope skin." Father Paul pulled the mask out of his bag to show to Alexander, who touched it gently.

Alexander's dream was interrupted by a female voice coming at him from above. "Drink, sir?" she asked. Alexander shook his head to clear it and opened his eyes. A flight attendant was standing in the aisle with a drink cart.

"Water, please, and two glasses of ice," Alexander replied. He remembered sitting at Father Paul's feet throughout the night while the missionary told him stories of Africa. Now he had seen it for himself.

Davenport, Iowa

It was an unusually hot April day with not a cloud in the sky. John stopped his combine and surveyed the wheat fields that had been in his family since the days of Abraham Lincoln. He had just planted twenty acres of wheat. He had rotated his crops and this year looked to be a good season for wheat. He wiped the sweat off his brow and stared at the blue spring sky. It had rained earlier, but now it was still and humid. He took another look at the sky and noticed some unusual clouds in the distance. Tonight was meatloaf night. That was Marge's specialty. She sure could make a mean meatloaf. Hoping those clouds didn't mean anything, he switched on the AM radio hanging from the gearshift to catch the weather report.

"Folks, there's been a malfunction in the weather reporting system we use," the announcer said. "Unfortunately we cannot give you an update, but out my window it looks clear and sunny."

The kids should be home from school now. *I do like that meatloaf,* he thought. He had another hour to go before dinner. He hoped the rain would hold off until he could make it home for dinner. *I don't like cold meatloaf,* he thought. A cold wind brushed his sweat-laden brow. The trees rimming the cleared field waved, mimicking the wave of the bleacher bums at a Cubs game. John was transfixed by their hypnotic dance, which turned frantic as the wind picked up. He heard what he thought was a freight train. John came out of his trance and realized that the low form in the distance was not rain, but a rotating transparent cloud beneath a dark mass of cloud and dust. Jumping off the combine, he ran for the house and yelled to his family to retreat to the cellar. His words were swept away by the swirling wind. The rotating cloud changed from its transparent mist to a solid brown mass at the edge of his fields. His combine was caught up and dropped thirty feet from where it had been. Trees snapped. Gasping, he made it to the house and watched his barn collapse like a house made of popsicle sticks. Livestock were impaled by the flying sheet metal. As he watched his livelihood destroyed in those few seconds, he wondered why there had been no warning.

University of Chicago, Illinois

"Jell-O, yes, banana pudding, yes, put a little more mashed potatoes on there. Salad, yes, hold off on the rice." Alexander carried his heavy tray through the cafeteria line in the dining room of the University of Chicago. "Hey, how about some of that chicken cordon bleu?" he said to the woman serving food behind the glass.

"Al, is there anything on the menu that you're not going to try?" A voice asked from behind him.

Balancing his tray, Alexander turned to look. His friend and colleague, Mike Hutchinson, was standing behind him. They had published papers on Aramaic and ancient languages together throughout grad school and were now both on tenure track at the world-renowned private university.

"Listen, for the last three months all I've eaten is beans and rice. I think I'm entitled to a little comfort food," Alexander said as he followed Mike to a table near the window and as far from the chattering noise of the students as possible. Looking around, Alexander noticed that very little conversation was actually taking place; most of the noise was texting or beeps signaling a new text message. He had forgotten these sounds after three months away from modern technology. The personal interaction of all the tribes made him realize how much was lost through this technology. The art of conversation was just that—an art that was seemingly forgotten back in this world.

"You look like you walked out of a World War II concentration camp." Mike's words drew him out of his trance. "How much weight did you lose?"

Alexander shrugged as he wolfed down his food. "Hey, if you're not going to eat that piece of cake, I'll take it," he said, savoring the chocolate cake his friend was picking at.

"When did you get in?" Mike handed him the cake. "I didn't see you at the faculty seminar last week."

"Last night. I was supposed to be in three days ago. I was detained in Nairobi while trying to get clearance to bring a kula back with me."

"Kula? What's that?

"It's a rain beetle."

"Tell me, since when do you care about bugs??"

"You don't understand. I was traveling all around southern Sudan and none of the 300 tribes shared the same words except for one."

"Let me guess—the kula."

"Yeah, and to top it off, some don't even have the 'k' sound in their language. We even found a picture of the kula on a cave wall. I took pictures. Here, look, let me show you." Alexander pulled out his iPhone from his back pocket. He brought up the photo gallery and handed it to his friend.

"This is amazing; I've never seen anything like it before." Mike said, his enthusiasm matching Alexander's as he studied the images of the cave drawings.

"From what I can make out, these pictures tell the history of the beetle. But the pictures don't follow any clear pattern and the words don't seem to explain the pictures. This might be a new language that has never been discovered. It could be just a start."

"That's amazing," Mike repeated.

Rebekah sat in the crowded lunchroom, trying to keep her attention focused on the new Danielle Steel novel, but her ears kept turning to the conversation at the next table. She was new at the University of Chicago and didn't know anyone. She was uncomfortable in new situations. Men were intimidated by her beauty and brains while women seemed jealous. She had become something of a loner. She didn't mind much. It allowed her to focus on her work.

"But the problem is I can't get a clear handle on it. These symbols pop up haphazardly and don't follow any clear pattern." Alexander shook his head, taking his phone back from his friend.

"That's the beauty of chaos," Rebekah said, not able to hold herself back any longer. Alexander and Mike both turned to look at a beautiful young woman sitting at the table next to them. Her skin was a translucent ivory, her hair a mass of auburn curls, her eyes a brilliant green. She was poking her head out from behind an iPad and eating a blueberry yogurt—part of which was still on her lip.

"Excuse me," Alexander said. "What did you say?"

Rebekah pulled her chair over by them and explained, "I couldn't help overhearing your conversation. There's a pattern to everything. If you're looking for the pattern though, you're not going to find it."

"Just who are you?" Mike asked.

"Rebekah Simmonds. I'm new here. I'm in the math department." She wiped the yogurt from her lips. "Mind if I take a look at these?" Without giving Alexander a chance to respond, she took the iPhone out of his hand and scrolled through the photo gallery. "Yeah, you're right. Looks like a combination of hieroglyphics and Aramaic."

Alexander looked surprised by her comments. "Math, huh?"

"I've studied ancient languages, but I don't recognize this one. What do you think these mean?" Rebekah stared at Alexander with an intensity that startled him.

"I think they're referring to the sun, or Rā, the Egyptian sun god. See this symbol here on the back of the cobra." Alexander used his two fingers to enlarge a photo so he could point to a symbol on the picture. It was a circle with two arrows drawn on the back of a cobra's hood. One arrow was pointing backwards, the other forwards. "I've never seen Rā symbolized with a snake. Egyptians identified snakes with Apepi, an evil god."

"How old did you say these drawings are?"

"I didn't. I have one small sample to carbon date but haven't had a chance to send it to the lab yet. That's my next stop," Alexander said, putting his phone back in his pocket. "The drawings have to be thousands of years old."

Rebekah shook her head. "Bizarre."

"What?"

"It's just bizarre. That symbol is the one used to explain the bipolar theory of events in chaotic math."

"What?"

"Chaotic math. It's my field of study." At their blank faces, Rebekah continued. "In chaotic math we solve problems using a bipolar theory. That means you start from the middle and move both ways." She pointed to the symbol. "Here, look at this. The circle represents us living in the now and how we move in two directions. The arrow pointing backwards is the past which is moving further away, and the one pointing forward is the future, which is coming closer."

Mike and Alexander looked at each other. Alexander scrolled through the camera gallery to enlarge a few more images. "Look, in some instances the symbol is reversed. Do you think they were using this to explain the past and the future?"

"Could be. See, everything is moving in two directions at the same time," Rebekah said, pushing her hair back from her face. "You're thinking with the western linear mind, but in chaotic math you need to let go of those thoughts and look at all sides as a continuum. Time doesn't end just because it's behind you."

"What did you say your name was?" Alexander asked, glancing at the clock on his phone, which was still acting crazy.

"Rebekah Simmonds." She held out her hand. "And you are?"

"Alexander Talcott," He shook her hand. "I'd like to continue our conversation, but I have to go teach a class." He stood up, lifting his tray. "Do you like Chinese food?"

Rebekah smiled. She turned and walked away. With one last look at Rebekah's retreating figure, Alexander headed through the courtyard and toward the university's Oriental Institute, home of the humanities program and setting for his upcoming language course.

This unseasonably warm April day reminded him of Sudan for a moment, except there was no cloud of dust, only the smell of engine exhaust. Instead of bugs chirping and mosquitoes buzzing, here he heard cars honking and multiple conversations as pedestrians talked on their cell phones. He had gone from one jungle to another. It reminded him of the book *Labyrinth of the Gods* with its composite of old world architecture and utilitarian design.

Students brushed past him on the way to their classes, going on to be doctors and lawyers. Very few would pursue the study of ancient languages. It was a science that didn't lend itself to prestige or big money. It was more of a calling than a career. His calling had come when he was a child. And his fascination had not diminished as he grew into a man, despite his father's attempts to talk him out of his path.

He walked into the classroom. Decorating the walls were maps of the world, showing both the new world and ancient civilizations. A podium stood at attention in the front of the room. In a semi-circle facing the podium was a wooden floor with benches on risers.

There were a handful of students, some trying to fill their humanities requirement, others in search of a major, and then there was Kenny. He had the calling. Tall and intellectual-looking with wire-rimmed glasses and a soft voice, Kenny spoke six languages, one of them being Klingon. He was going to carry the torch. Alexander relished their conversations even though Kenny could be a little demanding and needy.

Alexander set his briefcase on the old wooden desk and stood at the ancient wooden podium. The university used its funds on the more lucrative fields, particularly its world-class biological sciences division, not language.

"Welcome to Ancient Languages 2. I see some familiar faces, but for those who don't know me, my name is Professor Talcott. I'll pass out the syllabus for the class. You can find the reading materials listed on the website." Alexander handed out a few papers, which the students passed among the rows.

"As you can see, we're going to begin our year with a look at the ancient languages of Africa. Why Africa? Because that is where all languages stem from." Alexander leaned against his podium. He was back in his element—a musty room full of interested students. "I spent the last three months in southern Sudan, where there are at least 365 unwritten languages. I went to document them and hopefully catalog them so we could determine if there were any similarities between the languages. Could you imagine living in a United States where there were so many languages and no one could understand each other?"

A student whom Alexander recognized from the year before raised her hand. "Why are there so many?"

"The sub-Saharan landscape is harsh, and there is no infrastructure. For thousands of years the tribes lived separated by distance and culture. The heavy brush makes it difficult to travel from village to village," Alexander replied, gesturing with his hands as he spoke. "The tribes held onto their own lands, afraid of their warring neighbors, who would steal cattle and children. This kept conversation to a minimum." The class chuckled.

"When the Christians invaded Africa," Alexander continued, "they wanted to create a common bond to open the pathways to understanding and accepting the differences amongst the tribes. They brought the tribes together, but they also infected them with their diseases, their God, and their words. Now the old words are disappearing. They are not written down, and they are not being passed from generation to generation as they had been for thousands of years. English is the language of the future; it is the beginning of the end. Like all of the Earth's precious resources, languages are an endangered species. If we don't save them now, they will be lost forever; we have to understand where we come from before we can understand where we are going. After all, in the beginning was the word."

After class, Kenny watched several girls run up to the professor and ask him questions about Africa. He hated how they fawned over Professor Talcott. If they had been truly interested in language, he could excuse their sophomoric behavior. He waited for them to finish their babbling and then walked up to the professor.

"Kenny, it's good to see you." Alexander shook his star pupil's hand.

"Hi, Professor. I want to hear about your trip," Kenny said, sitting on the top of his desk. He listened intently while Alexander shared some of his recent experiences with the Sudanese people and their tribal customs.

"Wow, that's fascinating. How about dinner tonight? I can help you input all the data, and we can begin to categorize the languages," Kenny said. "I've been going through our old data files and I'm ready to begin work." Not only a language student, Kenny also was working an internship as Alexander's lab tech.

"That sounds great, Kenny. We'll have to make some time. Unfortunately I have a commitment tonight." Alexander said, opening his calendar on his phone.

"What about tomorrow night?"

"I've put that project on hold. With being gone so long, I haven't prepared for this semester, so I have to catch up and prepare lesson plans. Besides, I have another project to complete first."

"Is it something I can help with?" Kenny asked.

"We'll talk about it later. I have to prepare for my next class," Alexander said, closing his laptop case with a snap.

Kenny hesitated before standing up. Grabbing his backpack, he slowly walked out of the classroom.

Somewhere above Denver

Captain Ken Henderson tapped the altimeter. He was perplexed. He had been flying for twenty years and never had seen this problem before. All the instruments on the jumbo 777 were running backwards. Looking out the window, he could see they were flying level. He was maintaining a steady speed, but the panel was showing a drop in altitude.

His navigator came rushing into the cabin. "Captain, I've lost our bearings. All the instruments are going crazy. The GPS is out of whack. It has us somewhere north of England. We're actually only several miles from Denver International."

"We'll need to radio Denver to find out what's going on," the captain replied, reaching for the radio. "This is flight number 579. We're having instrument problems. Can you see our position?"

"All the systems are out," came the controller's voice through his headphone. "We're manually tracking airplanes and putting them into position. We'll need to put you on standby. Give us your position as close as possible."

Captain Henderson looked at his co-pilot, who was shaking in his boots. The captain shrugged off his concern. "This is nothing. In Iraq, I flew ground-level night sorties. It was pitch black with nothing but the mountaintops to guide us. We can handle this. Just like in Iraq, we have the mountains to guide us."

His copilot smiled a crooked, unsure smile and sank down into his chair.

Chinatown, Chicago

Alexander sat at the table of the Three Happiness restaurant in Chicago's Chinatown area. The restaurant was a landmark of both Chicago history and American-Chinese cuisine. He studied the menu while waiting for Rebekah to show up. His eye caught a woman coming in the door. Her long auburn hair was swirling around her shoulders, accenting a pair of emerald eyes and a heart-shaped face. Her voluptuous figure was not concealed by the jeans and oversized sweatshirt she wore. He finally realized it was Rebekah. He stood up and waved at her. "I'm over here."

Rebekah walked over and sat down across from Alexander. She smelled like magnolias and moonbeams, he thought. He had heard that phrase in a song once and always wondered what moonbeams would smell like. He had overheard his dad one time say his mom smelled like magnolias and moonbeams. He never quite knew what that meant until now. Chaotic math didn't seem so important anymore. She picked up a menu.

Taking his eyes off her, Alexander eyed the menu and thought about all his favorite dishes that he had missed while he was in Africa. Kung Pao chicken, Mongolian beef, shrimp with lobster sauce, fried rice. How could he pick just one? He hadn't been on a date in such a long time; he should show some restraint. But this wasn't really a date. "What will you have, sir?" the waiter asked, standing over the table, his pencil ready.

"I'll have the Kung Pao chicken, the Mongolian beef, and shrimp with broccoli." Alexander closed his menu, adding, "And don't forget the potstickers." Rebekah placed her order and the waiter walked away.

"Is someone else joining us for dinner?" Rebekah asked with a sarcastic grin.

"No, I've been eating beans and rice for the past three months and need to get it out of my system. I have a lot to make up for."

"Tell me about your time in Africa."

Alexander leaned back. "I received a grant to study the languages of the African tribes in sub-Saharan Africa."

"Why Africa?" Rebekah leaned her elbows on the table and stared at Alexander.

He was flattered by her interest. "There are more than 350 tribes and each one has their own language. I wanted to see if there are any similarities among them."

"Were there?"

"A few words were similar here and there, but not as many as you might think. That's why the rain beetle caught me off guard. You have to remember these languages are not written down. The name for the rain beetle, though, is the same in every tribe."

"What do you think it means?" Rebekah asked as their food arrived. She watched as Alexander devoured his three portions.

"I'm not quite sure," he said between bites.

"Maybe I can help you with that." She dipped a crab Rangoon into sweet and sour sauce before taking a bite.

"Any help would be appreciated."

"I've got a program that works like a template to help find correlations between unrelated information."

Alexander looked up from his plate. "Where do you find a program like that?"

"Actually I wrote it."

"You wrote it?" He waved his chopsticks in the air. "I'm impressed."

She shrugged. "It was part of my thesis."

"Do you think we could feed in my pictures from the cave?"

"We could certainly try. Look, I live ten minutes from here. We can go to my place and see if it would work with the pictures."

"Sounds great." Alexander handed her a fortune cookie from the tray and reached for the check.

She cracked the cookie open and pulled out the sliver of paper, "'Happiness is a two-way street,'" Rebekah read out loud and pulled out her wallet.

"Don't worry. This one's on me." Alexander waved her money aside.

They left the restaurant. "We can walk. My place isn't far from here," Rebekah said, leading the way. A few minutes later they arrived at an old warehouse that had been developed into trendy lofts. Its brick façade had been washed, but the new gleam couldn't overcome the dreariness of the barbed wire fence surrounding it. Alexander could never understand why people insisted on living in the heart of downtown. He followed her onto the elevator to the eleventh floor. Rebekah flung open the door to a spacious loft. Instead of retaining the original woodwork, the developer had updated using chrome. Boxes were piled all around the floor.

"Sorry about the mess. I just moved here and haven't had a chance to get organized yet," Rebekah said, taking her sweatshirt off and revealing a tight t-shirt.

Alexander swallowed hard and tried to avoid looking at her breasts. He watched her walk over to the computer, which was the only area that was completely organized. She flipped on the twenty-seven-inch monitor and an image of a circle with the two arrows appeared that resembled those he had seen in the cave. Alexander's mouth dropped. "Pretty spooky, huh?" Rebekah flashed him a smile as she sat in the leather chair at the computer table.

"That's strange," she said, peering closely at the computer.

"What's that?" Alexander sat on the edge of the couch so he could look over her shoulder.

"Look at the clock." She pointed to a corner of the screen. "It's running backwards."

"My phone's been like that for weeks. Have you heard anything about a virus?"

"No, I checked everything when I unpacked it, and with starting classes I haven't had any time to do any other work." She opened up the control panel and tried to change it. "This is even stranger. My clock is set to the atomic clock in Boulder, and it's never wrong. I'll fix it later."

She took out a white USB cord. "Hand me your phone. I'm going to download your photos," Rebekah said to Alexander. He handed her the iPhone, and she connected it via the USB to the computer. The computer quickly loaded the images to the drive. She moved them around the screen and brought them into the program, her hands were busy as she talked. "It's reading three different things," she said. "This seems to be one book of many. The middle part tells the story of the rain beetle and how it comes up from underground but will retreat under earth for the next fifty years. The first part tells about an extinct animal that I've never heard of before. The third part tells the future. It's some type of written language."

"Are you sure?"

"See, it shows this is now. This symbol represents the present by showing that beetle had just come out from underground." Rebekah pointed on the screen. "This shows that in the future the beetle will go back underground. History is moving backward and the future is continually changing because of the past."

"Huh?"

"It's hard to explain. We are always moving in two different directions in space." At Alexander's confused look, Rebekah tried to explain. "Take this rubber band." She pulled one off the desk. "If you stretch it two ways, what happens?"

"It snaps back."

"See, there's so much tension because the spring is tightening down on the other side. That's how time is in chaos. The past is pulling us back because the future can only stretch so far before the past affects its forward movement."

"I think I kind of get it."

"The problem with trying to understand your drawings is we think in linear thought. You have to open your mind and forget some of the ways you've been taught to think. That's where chaos comes in. It's been used to explain everything from God to space travel. Here in your drawings, they're obviously thinking in abstracts."

"What do you mean?"

"They were way ahead of their time. The drawings incorporate everyday events with future events. These drawings here talk of blood knowledge." She pointed to a series of drawings. "It says the blood of their ancestors tell them who they are. That it's not a magical howl at the moon, but there is a practical scientific blueprint to who they are."

"You're telling me they knew about DNA?" Alexander asked.

"That's not what they called it, but they understood that they carried their ancestors' bloodline." Rebekah turned around to look at him, a big smile on her face.

"This is amazing." Alexander smiled back at her.

She turned back to the computer. "If I'm reading this correctly, this has parts of many modern languages in it, but you would know better than me. Let me make you a printout." Rebekah pressed a key on the computer and paper spit into the printer tray.

"It's amazing." Alexander shook his head, thumbing through the pages as they came off the printer. "It seems to be some type of universal language."

"What do you mean?" Rebekah sat back in her chair and stretched her arms.

"Well." Alexander rubbed his head and tried to think of the best way to explain it. "It's kind of like Yiddish. It doesn't seem to be pure. It seems to be more bastardized. Bits and pieces of languages."

"That makes sense."

Alexander sank down on the couch again and studied the papers. "It really looks to be derived from a much more pure and highly sophisticated language that makes it possible to express such complex theories."

"We're limited because we're basing our assumptions on everything we've been taught. Most of the advances in science have been made by people who didn't realize they had limits. Galileo talked about air, stars, planets, space time, and travel long before he was tied down by scientific equipment." Rebekah continued. "Can you imagine if we were able to communicate our thoughts like this? Can you imagine the possibilities?" she asked, looking again at Alexander.

Sudan, Africa

Amat stepped over a spitting cobra larger than the one he had killed a few weeks ago. It was a good thing Alexander had left when he did. It was mid-April and the rain had drawn the snakes into the cave. They were everywhere, hissing and spitting, on the walls, the floor, and in some cases hanging from the ceiling. Now Amat was back in the cave with a team of archeologists from his own University of Nairobi. After Amat reported the drawings to the government, a team had been dispatched to excavate the drawings and search the cave to see if there were more.

"Mr. Amat, there's a secret passage that not even my grandfather knows about. There's more drawings in the passage." The boy hesitated. "My grandfather would be angry if he knew I went that far into the mountain," Kuot said, pointing to a long, narrow passageway.

"Take me there," Amat said, putting out his cigarette.

"I've never gone during the rainy season. Even during the dry season there's many snakes."

"Take me anyway," Amat repeated.

The gleam of Amat's flashlight bounced off the moist walls. Every crevice played home to a pair of split, yellow eyes. They treaded carefully, looking for both an even foothold and snakes. Even the sure-footed Africans found it difficult to navigate the narrowing uneven passageways. The echoes of the excavation team receded as they walked along the tight spaces deeper and deeper into the mountain. Amat thought about a movie he had seen when he was in university about a similar team that journeyed to the center of the earth. He half expected to see dinosaurs when they reached the end of their journey. Instead, he was surprised to enter a cavernous pit alive with a sea of writhing snakes. Their brown, wriggling bodies blurred into the deep brown sand under their feet. The boy stopped inches from falling into the pit. "I've never seen it this bad. The room is on the other side," he whispered. "This is as far as I go."

The floor dropped five feet—seven if you included the two feet of snakes. Shining his light along the side of the wall, Amat saw jagged rocks and holes that could serve as footholds. Amat saw no other choice. He ran his fingers over various parts of one and a stone pillar came up from the floor with a creaking noise. He tried a series of figures on the next drawing and another pillar came up. When he was done, there were seven pillars creating a footpath across the pit. "You wait here and shine your flashlight so I can see," he told the boy. With slow and steady movements, Amat walked along to the other side of the pit.

"I hope what's over there is worth this." Amat's words fell short to the hissing sound along the floor. Amat thought about Alexander and smiled.

He reached the precipice of the crevice walls, which jetted out five feet over the pit. Grateful for his new steel-toed boots, he kicked away some snakes before climbing through the hole.

Tokyo

Koji was eager to start his day. He donned his official jacket and stepped onto the floor of the Tokyo Stock Exchange. It was his first day on the trading floor, and he had been studying for years for this moment. He knew the stock market, and he was ready to start his career. He knew you could live or die in a matter of seconds on the floor. You had to be quick. On his way in, he had stopped at an altar to ask Buddha's blessing on this day. The temple was surrounded by April cherry blossoms. He felt invigorated, excited; this was his moment. The clock ticked the last few seconds to the opening bell. And then nothing. The awkward silence was broken by the TSE President Mr. Yoshimoto clearing his throat. His face was somber as he stood at the podium.

"Gentleman, I urge you to slowly and calmly contact your brokerage houses. All TSE and NASDAQ stocks trading information systems are down," Mr. Yoshimoto said.

"How can this be? How can every system be down? It's a failsafe system," Koji asked, his questions falling on deaf ears.

"We're working on the problem. Until then the TSE is closed. The SEC and other governmental agencies have put a freeze on buying and selling. All stocks are frozen at yesterday's prices. All mergers and acquisitions are on hold."

Koji stood still as there was a mass exodus of people pushing and pulling past him in a panic, reaching for their phones or moving out onto the street. He heard Mr. Yoshimoto turn to his assistant and say, "God help us. I've been here for thirty years and never seen anything like this."

Koji pulled out his cell phone. With a shaky hand, he attempted to call his supervisor. The first three tries resulted in a message saying the line was not working. Finally, on the fourth try, he got through. "Mr. Togo," he stammered into the phone.

"Koji, I heard. Our systems are down too."

"What do I do?" Koji asked, staring at the empty trading floor. This was not what he had expected. All his hard work and preparation had been for nothing.

"Go home and be with your family. And if you have anything in savings, I would suggest you get it out now. This could get worse."

"What is it? This is just temporary. It'll be fixed, right?" Koji said through his crackling phone.

"Go home and be with your family," his boss repeated.

Downtown Chicago

Now's the awkward moment, Alexander thought, standing in the doorway of Rebekah's loft, locked in the eternity between saying goodnight and actually leaving. Should he kiss her or shake her hand? He decided on the handshake, but when he extended his hand she pulled him in for a quick hug.

"Thanks for dinner. It was great, and thanks for letting me in on your project," she said.

"Thanks for your help. See you at school tomorrow." As he walked back to his car, he saw the reflection of the moon in a puddle. The air was cool following the slight April rain. It made for a pleasant night as he thought about moonbeams and smiled.

Alexander walked up the three steps to his house, looking forward to his nice, warm bed. He was still coming down from the high of being with Rebekah when a voice from the shadows startled him. His heart pounding, he turned to see a figure come out from behind the bushes. It took him a moment to recognize the figure.

"Kenny? What are you doing here?" Alexander asked.

"Professor Talcott, I know it's late. I've been working on the project. I've got some great ideas. I thought we could make some time to go over things."

"Now?" Alexander asked, fiddling with his keys. He heard the phone ringing. He looked at his watch. It was two a.m. At this time of night, the phone only rang with bad news. He went through his mental contact list of his relatives who were sick or old as he flung the door open. He reached for the doorknob and looked back at Kenny, not wanting to be rude.

"Come in for a minute," he said, rushing into the house. He grabbed the phone on the fourth ring. "Hello," he said in a breathless voice.

"Hello, my friend," echoed a voice through a very staticky line.

"Amat, is that you?" Alexander breathed a sigh of relief. Amat had probably forgotten about the nine hours that separated Chicago from Nairobi.

"Yes, Alexander, my friend. I have exciting news."

"What is it?"

"I've been back to the cave. We found more drawings and six scrolls. I've copied the pages and emailed them to you."

Alexander struggled to hear Amat's words. His voice crackled in and out. "What's that?" He practically shouted into the phone.

"I emailed you some pages."

"Did you say email?"

"Yes, your email on the computer. Check it."

Holding the phone to his ear, Alexander ran up the stairs to his office. He looked at his computer to see the tiny envelope in the corner indicating new mail. He signed on and opened the mail.

"I've got them." He looked at the images on screen and pressed the print button. "Where are you now? Can I reach you?"

"I'm calling from Loki. I'll call you when we return to Nairobi."

"I can't hear you clearly."

"Yes, the phone lines have been very bad. I will call you when I return to Loki," Amat shouted.

Alexander heard a faint click followed by a dial tone. He sat in his chair to study the drawings and almost fell backward in his seat. The images were amazing.

"What's that?" Kenny asked, looking over his shoulder.

Alexander put the images face down on his desk. "Nothing. Some things I'm working on." He brushed off Kenny's questions. He swiveled his chair around to talk to Kenny. "Kenny, I told you earlier our project is going to have to be on hold for a while. I'm busy with my classes, and I have some things I need to address."

"Things or people?" Kenny asked.

"Excuse me?" Alexander looked at him.

"Nothing. I'll go now. I'll show myself out." Kenny walked down the stairs. Alexander followed him, wanting to make sure the door was locked behind him.

"I'll see you in class," Alexander said.

Kenny nodded his head and walked down the steps. *Project, huh,* he thought. He had watched the professor at the restaurant and then later at her apartment.

Alexander bolted the door behind him and ran back up the stairs. He studied the images and longed to go back to Africa to see it with his own eyes. It was a room perhaps 100 feet square. It had symmetrical corners and benches cut out of stone walls. There were cabinets. On top of the cabinets were clay pots and jars. Some lay broken on the floor. Man had definitely known this place. What added to his certainty were the hundreds of skeletons that were strewn about the floor and on the benches. There were swords and shields as if they had been prepared for a battle with an imaginary enemy. Huddled in a corner lay the skeletal remains of children.

Why would a group of people choose such a remote place to be? Alexander mused. He lined the pictures up on his desk and studied them. There appeared to have been enough food to last a long while. The pages copied from the book were in the same unusual combination of hieroglyphics, Hebrew, Sumerian, and Aramaic. He located the curious symbol on a page and circled it to show Rebekah. One page of illustrations appeared to depict fighting, though it was hard to tell. Alexander squinted. These email images were so grainy. Maybe these people were in hiding. The images stayed with him even as he shut his eyes. Scenarios played through his head of what happened in that room so many years ago. As he drifted off, he heard the rattle of bones and the clash of metal.

Mozambique

Bruce had been up for twenty-four hours monitoring the dam near the Limpopo River in Mozambique. This year's rainy season was heavier than usual; much of Africa was being hit hard. Part of Bruce's job as chief engineer was to make sure the water pressure behind the dam stayed within safe limits. The last twenty-four hours had brought an unusual deluge of torrential rain. The natural water system had been down for days now. Bruce walked the catwalk that ran the length of the dam checking the turbines, which powered the surrounding countryside. He took great pride in his dam. It was a pilot project—nearly ninety-eight percent automated. All systems were regulated by a special computer program that Bruce had helped develop. It still required a human touch to check the gauges and levels in case of any malfunction. The computer adjusted for back pressure on the wall and opened valves to allow enough water through to keep both sides of the dam at acceptable levels. So far all was well, especially considering it was the rainy season.

Bruce passed the coffee machine. He paused for a moment but after thinking, he decided a nap would be better. Fifteen minutes should be enough to keep him going until the morning crew arrived. When his head hit the pillow, he was out. If he had looked at the computer before closing his eyes, he would have noticed the clock running backwards and known something was wrong. Instead he was sound asleep, dreaming about his home in Jasper, Wyoming. He had been in Africa for two years as part of the Army Corps of Engineers. But Jasper seemed a lifetime away. He was still sleeping when the computers went down and shut the emergency valves. He was dreaming about horseback riding when the pressure built so high the dam finally burst. And then his dreams were over forever.

Chicago

The next morning, Alexander woke up with a stiff neck. He had fallen asleep in his office chair while studying the images. No new conclusions had entered his mind, but he couldn't wait to show the pictures around school and hear other theories. Though if he didn't get moving he wouldn't have time for anything other than going straight to class.

As Alexander moved toward the front door, his house phone rang. He ran to answer it. "Hello."

"Alexander, it's Dad," the voice said from the other end of the phone.

"Dad, I'm sorry. I meant to call you when I got back. I've been so busy getting ready for classes."

"I'd like to hear about your trip. I'm flying into O'Hare on Sunday. Can we meet for dinner?"

"That sounds great, Dad. Can I call you back? I gotta go now but we can talk later." Alexander hung up the phone.

Washington, DC

Colonel Talcott put down the phone slowly and returned to his desk at the Pentagon. Things were moving quickly now and he was concerned for Alexander. His security clearance had given him just enough priority to know that he had to prepare for large troop movement heading out to Egypt.

As quartermaster, he could tell what kind of trouble it was by the equipment that was ordered up, and this was bad—really bad. There was a lot of chemical and radiation protective gear being loaded on the C130s. He sank down into his chair and looked at the picture of Alexander and his wife, Katie. The photo was taken before the cancer took Katie.

He put a Macanudo cigar in his mouth and resisted the urge to light it up. For now, he just chewed the edges off until he could get to a place that allowed cigar smoke. Not too many of those places were around anymore. Everyone was so worried about secondhand smoke, but if they knew what was coming, secondhand smoke didn't seem so bad.

Oakland, CA

The temperature outside was reaching 100 degrees, not typical of April in northern California. The BART car was crowded, hot, and smelled of sweat and stale air. Inside, a group of teenagers wearing Giants shirts were talking loudly about the upcoming game. A young couple made out on the handicapped seat. On the other side of the aisle, a professionally dressed woman wiped the sweat off her made-up face and held onto her protruding belly. Several business people clutched their suitcases as the train bounced along the tracks.

Susan sat quietly, observing the other passengers, preparing herself for the four-mile journey, 135 feet under the San Francisco Bay. She had spent years in therapy to deal with her claustrophobia and her agoraphobia. She had been out of work for almost a year, but today she had an interview for a new job. There were only two ways to get there, and her car had been repossessed. Her house was next.

As she watched the rowdy teenagers, she clenched her fists; her knuckles were white. She kept repeating to herself, "I can do this."

The train ventured into the underground tunnel, her mouth went dry. She tried desperately to bring up enough saliva to swallow. Her heart was pounding. Everyone else seemed oblivious as they continued texting and talking. To them, it was just another train ride.

She felt the pressure of thousands of tons of water above her head, squeezing the air out of the train compartment. She had enacted this scenario over and over in her therapist's office. She tried the slow breathing techniques that the doctor had taught her. Her heart continued to pound out of her chest. It had to be at least two minutes—it couldn't be much longer. Had it been a mile, two miles?

The overhead lights flickered on and off for a quick second. Her breathing stopped. And then came the horrifying squeal of metal on metal as the train screeched to a halt. The car went dark.

Chicago

Alexander grabbed his wallet and took a quick peek inside. It was empty. The Chinese dinner had wiped out the last of his cash left from his trip. He would have to stop at the ATM on his way to class. He drove up to the machine thinking how decadent and spoiled Americans were. Drive-through cash machines, drive-through dinners, drive-through cleaners, drive-through prescriptions. Soon there would be no reason to ever leave your car. It was nothing like the desolate landscape of Africa where there were not even roads. He inserted his card and punched in his PIN. The machine gave him a message saying it was an invalid PIN. He tried again. Same message. On the third try, the machine sucked in his card. He pounded on the machine. Not again. This was the fifth card he had been through. Not a good start for the day. Alexander parked his car and walked to the bank entrance. There was a line of people gathered in front all talking loudly. He noticed his neighbor in the front of the line.

"Hey, Mr. Sneed, what's going on?" Alexander said, glancing at his phone.

Mr. Sneed tapped on his watch. "The damn thing hasn't worked in days."

"Same with the clock on my phone."

"I haven't seen you since you got back. Haven't you heard the news or read the paper?"

"No, I haven't even turned my TV on yet."

"Some kind of virus has knocked out the stock exchange. People are afraid their bank records will be next. I haven't seen a panic like this since black Friday in 1987."

"What do you mean?" Alexander asked.

"It looks like a crash to me. And I bet it could be worse than the one of 1987."

"But our money's insured." Alexander pointed to the FDIC sticker on the bank window.

"That doesn't mean anything. I'm still getting my money out."

"I'm just here because the ATM ate my card."

"All the ATMs are down."

"What, at this bank? They have lousy service here. I'm only here because it's between work and home."

"No, everywhere."

The doors to the bank opened and people rushed in. Alexander looked at the crowd and knew he would never make it to class on time if he stayed. On his meager teacher's salary, he didn't have much to lose. Most of his funds were tied up in the teacher's credit union. He would stop there at lunch. He headed back to his car.

Alexander walked into the cafeteria hoping Annie was working. If she was, he could probably charm her into letting him pay later. He really needed a cup of coffee. "Good morning" a voice called to him from across the room.

He looked over and saw Rebekah waving and walking towards him. "Morning," he replied. "You want to join me for a cup of coffee?"

"Sure." She gave him a big smile.

"Do you mind treating?" Alexander asked, shoving his hands into his jeans pockets.

"No, you paid for dinner last night."

"I stopped at the ATM and the machine ate my card." He followed her over to the coffee bar.

"Isn't it something?" Rebekah turned and asked him after ordering a tall cappuccino with extra whipped cream. "Our operating systems are breaking down everywhere. It's all over the news."

After she paid for their coffee, he followed her over to an empty table near the window. Usually the cafeteria at this time was bustling with people. That was not the case today. Alexander looked around and then back at Rebekah. "Looks like it's going to be a pretty light day."

"I know. I heard that half the staff called in, and so did a lot of the students," she said as she stirred her coffee. "I found out what the problem was with my computer clock. The atomic clock is out in Boulder. It's tied in with the ATMs being down."

"I'm sure they'll get it fixed." Alexander shrugged his shoulders. So far none of it had really affected him.

"After you went home, I tried working the drawings to see if I could find any more information, but my program went nuts. My version still has some bugs that I have to fix. I don't have the original program. I was hoping to try it in the computer lab here, but I heard these systems are down, too."

"That's too bad. Last night when I got home I had a call from Amat." At her blank look, he explained. "Amat was my guide in Africa. My partner. He emailed me these." Alexander took the printed pages out of his backpack and handed them to her. "These are more drawings that were deeper in the cave."

She studied the drawings. "This is unbelievable. What do you think happened? All these people. How tragic." She shook her head.

"I don't know yet. The pictures are pretty grainy. I did recognize some of the urns and jars as Mesopotamian. They appear to be from about the same period as some of the drawings in the front of the cave. I have a friend at the Field Museum and plan to stop by there and show him." Alexander glanced at his phone only to realize that the clock still wasn't working. He finished his coffee.

"Mind if I tag along?"

"Please do."

"How'd he find this?" Rebekah leafed through the pages.

"I'm not quite sure. We lost our phone line. He's going to call me back after he gets back to the university. I'll find out more then. Well, we better get to class. That is, if there is a class," he said half-joking. They both laughed and stood up.

"Which way are you going?" Alexander asked, as they walked out of the cafeteria.

"I'm going that way." Rebekah pointed toward the city skyline.

"Too bad. I'm going the other way," Alexander said. "How 'bout if we meet here after class? Around noon."

She nodded her agreement. "See you then." Watching Rebekah walk away, he realized it wasn't just good food, beer and music that he missed while in Africa. Spending time with her reminded him how long it had been since he was with a woman. It wasn't that women didn't find him attractive—quite the opposite. He had his share of casual sex, but he was looking for more than that. He was looking for someone he could talk to.

It was a short morning. All classes were cancelled due to the computer problems and the run on the banks. Alexander met Rebekah in front of the cafeteria, a full hour earlier than they had anticipated. They talked as they walked to his car. "I need to stop at the credit union. I hate not having some cash," Alexander said as he drove away from the university.

"I heard everyone was going there," Rebekah said, putting on her seatbelt. "It's really turning into a panic." She eyed the streets, which were crowded with people leaving office buildings and classrooms. Most people looked uncertain and hesitant as they scurried through the city streets.

"There's nothing we can do about it. They'll get it fixed," Alexander said with a confidence he didn't quite feel.

"These pictures are really haunting," Rebekah said, pulling them out of Alexander's backpack. "I've had all these thoughts going through my head. I think about Masada, Jamestown, or Jonestown. The part that really makes me sad is the small skeletons you see huddled together. All the swords and spears toward the entrance. It looks like they were fighting off somebody." Rebekah shivered.

"I think it was their last bastion. I think my friend Lloyd may have some insight. This is his thing."

They pulled up in front of the credit union. It was packed and a line had formed outside the door. People were being turned away. As Alexander got out of the car, he saw Mike. "Hey Mike, what's going on?"

Mike walked over to him. "Forget it. Don't even try it. The credit union is out of money."

"Don't joke with me. What is it, a run on the bank, Mr. Potter?"

"No, I'm not kidding around. They're literally out of money. Everyone is out of money," Mike said with a serious face.

"Out of money? What do you mean?" Alexander asked.

"They're giving out vouchers. They have no money on site." Mike shook his head. "This is bad, really bad. I've got a couple hundred stashed at home. I'm going to stock up on food and just stay home with the kids."

"C'mon, Mike, you're feeding into the frenzy. That attitude is what starts mass hysteria. When people start hoarding, the food supply goes low."

"Take a look around. What do you think we have now?"

Alexander looked around at the people clamoring outside the credit union entrance and milling around the streets. He looked at Rebekah. He got back into the car and headed over to the Field Museum.

"I'm really getting worried," she said, turning on the radio.

"There has been looting reported on Michigan Avenue," the announcer's voice said in a frantic, excited tone. "If you don't have a reason to leave your house, our advice is don't. A federal state of emergency has been declared, and the governor has called up the National Guard..." The announcer's voice continued until Alexander turned the radio off.

"It may not be safe to be out," Rebekah said, looking around at the crowded streets.

"We're ten minutes from the museum. If I know Lloyd, he's there no matter what."

Alexander was surprised to find a parking space in front of a meter on the circle drive that surrounded the museum. He and Rebekah knocked on the door to the main entrance, which was locked.

A guard came over and waved them away. Alexander pounded on the door. "Go away, the museum's closed," the guard said through the glass pane.

"Listen, I'm a friend of one of the curators."

"There's no one here," the guard replied.

"No, Lloyd will be here. He lives here. It's urgent. Please let us in," Alexander pleaded.

Rebekah smiled at the guard. Slowly turning his key, the guard let them in. Their footsteps echoed through the empty main hall. They followed the hallway to the special exhibit of the Dead Sea Scrolls. They stopped for a moment and stared into the glass case. Shivers ran up their backs as they marveled at these historic documents. Looking around, Alexander spotted Lloyd standing by one of the panes. He was wearing dirty jeans and a t-shirt that said, "What the hell are you looking at?" Lloyd had been born and raised along Chicago's wealthy North Shore. He gave up old money for old bones. He had told Alexander that when his parents had died in a plane crash, they had left an estate worth $200 million. It didn't affect Lloyd either way, except he did buy an awesome four-seater Cessna. If there was one thing Lloyd loved as much as archeology, it was flying.

The pair had formed a bond while at Sidwell Friends School in Washington, DC. Both had been outsiders— Alexander, shy and quiet, while Lloyd was loud and known as a troublemaker. Lloyd's father made his fortune as a contractor selling high-end technology parts to the military. That's where he met Alexander's dad; the boys were forced to spend time together, and they wound up best friends.

"Hey, Bone Digger," Alexander called over to him.

Lloyd looked around the exhibit. "Alexander the Great. What are you doing here?" He walked over to his friend.

"I need your help with something. By the way, this is Rebekah."

Lloyd smiled and looked her up and down with the usual reaction that men gave her. She was used to it, but it still gave her a kick. "Nice to meet you," Rebekah said, holding out her hand.

Lloyd wiped his hand on his jeans and shook hers. "You guys haven't seen the exhibit yet?" Lloyd walked over to the display case. "Just imagine. 2,000 years ago Christ walked the earth and these were his words to his scribes. It's amazing to think of the power that the written word has."

Alexander and Rebekah looked at each other. "That's kind of what we're here about."

Alexander told Lloyd about his trip to Africa and the cave. Rebekah placed her hands on the Plexiglas-covered scrolls and let the power of the artifact consume her. She imagined the great teacher standing before his disciples and what it might be like to hear the voice of God. She wondered what his voice sounded like. She had an image of Charlton Heston standing before the burning bush and wondered if Hollywood had gotten it right. She shook her head.

Alexander was saying, "These are the emails I got from Amat." He showed the original pictures and the emailed ones from Amat.

"This is an incredible find. Do you know what you have here?" Lloyd asked.

"As far as I can tell, the pots and urns look like Mesopatamian."

"Definitely influenced. If you notice, some aren't clay, they're alabaster, which would make them Egyptian. Look at the spear tips, how precisely they're tooled. It's hard to tell from these pictures. The sheen on them looks metallic. If you want to leave these with me, I'll look them over."

"I was trying to plug them into a program on my computer, but for some reason it's not working. I have a program called a chaotic correlator that looks for similarities between different items. It has a very robust database," Rebekah said.

"Rebekah teaches math at the U of C," Alexander interjected.

"Chaotic math. I've read about that. They tried using it to explain the Book of the Dead," Lloyd said.

"How does chaotic math explain the Book of the Dead? They're not even related," Alexander asked.

"Remember that Egyptian nobility would be buried with things from this world so they could take them with them to the next world. Come here." Lloyd walked down a long, dark corridor. He led them into the Egyptian exhibit room. Behind a case was a long scroll. "There. That's a Book of the Dead. Starting at the beginning." He led them along the encased exhibit of the scroll. "The person dies and is embalmed. Then they go before the judges and the scale of justice. If they succeed in judgment, they move onto the next world. If not, they die a terrible second eternal death. See how your past continues to affect your future."

As they looked at the scroll, Rebekah saw the sign of the sun with the two distinct arrows. "Wait." She pointed to the small section.

"What's wrong?" Lloyd and Alexander came to stand behind her and looked at where her finger was pointing.

"It looks similar to the drawings on the cave," Rebekah said.

"I'm not surprised. The Nubians and Egyptians split off from that area. The Nubians went south and the Egyptians north. It's only natural that they have some similarity in culture," Lloyd said.

"But it's also the symbol we use in chaotic math."

"Are you saying that this Egyptian symbol inspired the chaotic math symbol?" Lloyd asked.

"No, that's the part I don't understand." Rebekah shook her head. "We just developed it because it's the most basic way to explain the theory. We thought that we invented that symbol."

"Apparently not." Lloyd paused. "I always think better on a full stomach. Let's go get a bite and a beer," Lloyd said. "I know a great place."

They all crowded into Lloyd's Pathfinder and drove a short distance to Rocky's Bar. Wedged under the Chicago skyline are several narrow bars—one of them, Rocky's. It had a cool, dark interior welcoming them from the hot sun. Its hardwood floors dated back to the Chicago fire, and Rocky, the bartender, was nearly as old.

"Hey, Rock." Lloyd waved to the bartender and held up three fingers indicating three beers. There was no need to say what kind. Rocky's only had one draft beer—Budweiser, the brew of the nearby Chicago Cubs. If anyone wanted any imported stuff, they'd have to buy it by the bottle and Rocky would give it to them with a disapproving look on his face.

They picked a table in the corner away from the regulars holding up the bar. The television was tuned in to the Cubs game. The drone of the announcer served as background noise. Lloyd took out the pictures and looked them over again.

"These jars are definitely from the Mesopotamian region," Lloyd said, pointing to some detail on the pictures. "I would say they were somewhere around 6,000 years old, but the armor and weapons are another thing. It almost seems like they are two different eras."

Alexander nodded his head in agreement. "That's the problem—" The rest of his sentence was interrupted by one of the barflies shouting, "Turn it up, turn it up." The three turned toward the television to see what the noise was about.

An announcer came onscreen and said, "We turn to the president, who is being broadcast live from the Oval Office."

The screen flashed to the Oval Office. The president, a distinguished-looking gentleman in his fifties with graying hair, was sitting behind his desk.

"My fellow Americans." He spoke slowly and deliberately. "We are in a time of crisis. I want to reassure you we are working on solving the problems that we are all facing. We are going to get things working again. There is no cause for panic. The finest minds in the country are at work to find a solution to fix the problems that are occurring with some of our communication systems. We are in control of the situation. Once again, there is no need to panic. This situation will be resolved quickly. Until then, I ask for your help. There have been some reports of hoarding and price fixing. I have passed an emergency edict freezing prices on gas, food, and medical supplies. I ask that we all work together. Help your neighbors, especially the older folks and those with impairments. We must come together as a nation. To ensure peace during this crisis, I have issued the order for martial law to be enforced by any state so choosing. Curfews will be set according to state legislation, and I ask that everyone cooperate with their local law enforcement agencies. We will keep you informed of our progress."

The screen returned to the announcer, who analyzed the president's address. "It doesn't look good, does it?" Rebekah asked, turning to face Lloyd and Alexander.

Both men nodded their heads in agreement. They finished their hamburgers in silence. When the waitress returned to clear their dirty plates, she also brought three slices of apple pie. Rebekah and Alexander didn't want any, so Lloyd wolfed down all three pieces.

Rebekah chuckled in amazement. "Where do you put that?"

"It's my one weakness. Pie. I can't get enough of it," Lloyd responded. "How 'bout another pitcher?" Lloyd asked. "If we're going down, we might as well have a buzz on."

Alexander smiled. Beer was Lloyd's answer to all of life's little problems. "How did you two meet?" Rebekah asked.

"We both went to the same prep school. Al was a real loser. I took him under my wing," Lloyd said.

"Me? The only thing missing from you was a pocket protector," Alexander replied.

Lloyd laughed. "He was kind of a dork. I took pity on him. I would take him to the different parties and introduce him to girls. I'd tell them how he rode the special yellow bus to school." Alexander rolled his eyes.

"What about you, Becky? What school did you go to?" Lloyd said with a slur.

"Becky. I haven't been called Becky since I was nine. I started at Brown University and did my graduate work at Oxford, and then the University of Glasgow."

"Oxford? Is that a community college? I've never heard of it," Lloyd teased.

"No, Lloyd, that's where people go when they can't get into U of I," Alexander retorted, teasing Rebekah.

The afternoon trickled away as they exchanged stories about their college days. The bar was a sanctuary from the turmoil going on in the world around them. Their laughter stopped when the television volume increased.

They looked at the television screen and saw a local reporter standing on Chicago's famous Magnificent Mile. The camera showed people behind her breaking the store windows of Neiman Marcus, Nike, and Bloomingdale's. They were running with as many items as their hands could carry and pushing and jostling into the reporter, who was struggling to maintain her bearing. She lost it and disappeared into the crowd.

Lloyd looked over at Alexander and sang, "'It's the end of the world as we know it.'" The whole bar joined in the singing until the harsh shrill of an emergency siren drowned them out. They turned the TV volume back up. Images of looting and rioting appeared behind the head of a local television newscaster. "We go now to the governor in Springfield."

The governor appeared on the screen. He had a somber look and was holding a sheet of paper, which he read from. "To ensure your safety, I have spoken with the president and have decided to declare a state of martial law throughout Illinois. From now until the situation is resolved, there is a dusk-to-dawn curfew. This curfew will be strictly enforced. Anyone on the street after six p.m. will be arrested. I urge you to stay in your homes and stay tuned for updates. We're all in this together. If everyone cooperates, with God's help, we will be fine. Thank you."

The newscast returned to the announcer. "Some businesses in the city and suburbs will remain open during this crisis." She read a list as the reporter's ghostly image faded away like a vapor trail etched into the LED screen. The TV screen went black.

"It doesn't sound like the city will be the safest place to be tonight. Why don't you guys come out to my farm? It'll be much safer, and it's well stocked. After all, Al, you knew my dad. We'll be safe there." Lloyd paid their bill.

Alexander and Rebekah looked at each other and then both agreed to go with Lloyd. As they left the bar, they were swept up into a crowd of looters. Chicago cops on horseback were pushing people into a circle. The cops on their steeds surrounded the people like it was roundup time at the Southfork Ranch. At either end of the street, military vehicles blocked off the exits. National Guardsmen wearing full combat gear were arbitrarily grabbing people and loading them into trucks.

As they stepped off the sidewalk from the bar, Alexander turned to Lloyd and said, "All that's missing are swastikas!"

Before he could reply, Lloyd was hit on the shoulder by a nightstick; the pain exploded and spiraled through his nervous system until he thought he would faint. Instead he fell to the ground and vomited.

"Lloyd!" Alexander reached down and pulled up his friend. "We have to get out of here." He turned to look for Rebekah. The only glimpse he caught of her was a flash of auburn hair being shoved into a truck. "Becky!" he cried, but his voiced was silenced by the maddening screech of the sirens.

The truck took off, as Alexander stood amongst the lowest of human misery. Some lay wounded in the street; others were being sent off to an unknown fate. He watched the taillights fade into the night, vanishing into the dark. And with them went the first casualty of war—freedom.

Glasgow, Scotland

"Done," Angus declared as he pushed his opponent's arm down onto the table. It was closing time at the High Road Pub, and he had time for one more victory drink. He was three kilts to the wind and he was preparing for the long stumble home. He had a room on campus, which was a convenient walking distance to the pub and his classes, too. But his real work was done high up in the hills.

He finished his drink and was the last one out before the bartender locked the door. If he had been a little less drunk, he would have been able to fend off his attackers. He didn't see the black van pull up until it was too late. Two men in dark suits hit him with a Taser and then threw him in the back of the van. The van took off with a screech. He was high on the most wanted list of the Forced Volunteer Agency (FVA).

Chicago

Rebekah looked around the interior of the truck. Her traveling companions were an eclectic group. There were stockbroker and lawyer types clad in Armani, Versace, and Polo. Their once-crisp suits were now tattered and bloodstained. There were gang members wearing their colors. Yet they too bore red splotches. It was the one thing they all bore in common—the color red.

Rebekah felt a trickle run down the side of her face. Luckily for her, the baton had been wielded by a rookie guardsman who gave her a glancing blow along the side of her head. A seasoned guard would have sent her to the emergency room.

"What are you looking at?" A young Latino man moved inches from Rebekah's face.

"Nothing. I am just a little disoriented," she replied with a whimper and a shake of her head.

"I think she likes you, Paco," another gang-banger said with a heavy Spanish accent.

"Is that true, *mija*? Do you want to dance with the devil?" The first man danced in front of her. "I am Diablo, you know, the one who you see walking towards you and then you cross the street. You lock your car doors when you drive through my hood on the way to your big fancy houses! There's no car doors to lock in here, *puta*!" With his final word he grabbed for Rebekah's blouse. Before she could react, the man clad in Armani cold-cocked Paco with a right hook. Just as the rest of the gang moved in, the truck halted with a screech, throwing them back against the wall. The doors flew open.

"Exit the truck one at time, keep your hands behind your head, and no talking," said the soldier standing at the back of the truck. He was not National Guard. They had been wearing the green and brown camouflage of the regular army. This soldier was geared in gray; the only other color was a blue patch that Rebekah could not make out. He pointed his M-16 at them as they exited the truck.

Rebekah turned to the man who had rescued her. "Thank you; my name is Rebekah."

"I'm Steven. I would shake your hand except I am afraid Rambo over there might put a bullet in me," he said.

Rebekah smiled. She waited for the usual return that she got from men, but Steven did not seem affected.

"I stopped off for a few after work to let the traffic die down; we broke early today," he chattered, as if oblivious to her charm. "I work for the Merc, in IT. I handle international trades; there's a bit of a bug in the system I've been working on."

Rebekah shivered as the cool dusk air stemming from the lake hit her. She looked around. The truck had pulled up to the south entrance of Soldier Field. This Sunday the Bears would not be playing; instead, the football stadium had been turned into a temporary holding facility. The soldiers marched the prisoners through the worn pillars of the sacred building. At one time, heroes with names like "Fridge" and "Sweetness" charged the field through these very same pillars. Now there were no heroes, just victims.

The gray uniforms were everywhere. Makeshift tents with cots were set up on the field, which was surrounded by a chain link fence topped with barbed wire.

"Have your IDs out, and walk on the yellow line to the first table; do not step off the yellow line, do not talk." The soldier they had nicknamed Rambo blurted out his commands with assured authority. He was not joking. Rebekah walked the line, followed by Steven.

"Follow the yellow brick road," she whispered back to her new friend.

"I don't think we're in Kansas anymore, Dorothy," he replied.

Field Museum, Chicago

Pushing through the crowd, Alexander and Lloyd managed their way back to the Field Museum. It was in view of Soldier Field. The two sat on the steps and watched the wagon train of gray military vehicles as they paraded up Lake Shore Drive on their way to the Stadium.

"I bet that is where they took Becky," Lloyd said, rubbing his still throbbing shoulder. "I don't like the color of those trucks."

"What do you mean?" Alexander replied.

Lloyd stood up and paced in front of Alexander. "You can tell what type of war the army is preparing for by the color of their gear. In Vietnam it was jungle warfare, so everything was green and brown camo; in the Gulf war it was sandy yellow. Now look at them, Al; who do think they are preparing to fight? What battlefield is gray?"

Alexander shrugged his shoulders.

"Urban warfare, Al; these streets—our streets—are the next battlefield!" Lloyd sat down next to Alexander and continued in a lowered voice as though someone else might be listening. "I have a friend who works out at Fermilab; you don't hear much about what goes on out there. The government set it right in the heart of suburbia. It's like they are saying, 'Hey look at us, nothing to hide here, just your neighbors looking for alternative sources of energy, we might even stop by to borrow a cup of sugar'—a cup of anthrax, more likely!"

"What are you talking about, Lloyd? Are you trying to tell me that the government is doing covert biological research a mile away from the strip mall?"

"Hide in plain sight, Al. How do you think that the CIA walks among us? They aren't wearing little American flag pins and holding one hand to an ear piece! They are Joe Schmoe, sitting on the bar stool next to you, listening to you complain about your taxes and taking notes!"

Lloyd had a conspiracy theory fetish, but as Alexander watched the constant cavalcade of gray military vehicles rush by, he listened to Lloyd with a new intensity. "Anyway, my friend comes to see me about a week ago; he tells me that the army is stockpiling equipment on the compound. He says all the gear is gray, and that the soldiers are wearing the quail's egg blue patch of NATO. And get this—they have raised a NATO flag and it's flying above the American flag! It is the new world order. It started when Nixon opened up China—" His words were interrupted by Alexander.

"Hold on; you had me until you mentioned Nixon, Lloyd." Alexander lessened the intensity of his attention; this was a worn out theory of Lloyd's. Usually it took a lot of shots of Jack Daniels to drag out Nixon.

"Hear me out," Lloyd continued. "Nixon opens up China and suddenly the world seems a little smaller. Next thing you know, the Berlin Wall is tumbling down while Roger Waters and Pink Floyd are playing to a MTV audience around the world! Ten years later, Europe unites and introduces the Euro-Dollar. And now the American flag is flying under the New World Order flag! My dad, and yours too, Al, fought for that American flag."

Alexander thought about his dad stationed in Washington; he would not salute any flag but Old Glory. "Lloyd, I think that we need to discuss the matter at hand; if they did take Becky to Soldier Field, how are we going to get her out?"

Lloyd sat and thought for a moment. And then inspiration struck. He jumped up, heading around the side of the building. "Follow me." Taking a large key chain off his belt loop, Lloyd opened an almost invisible steel door hidden by the limestone of the museum's side exterior.

Alexander followed him as they walked past the empty entryway. As they walked, the door slammed with a large thud that reverberated throughout the corridor. Their footsteps echoed with an eerie hollowness that filled the cavernous hall that stretched up hundreds of feet. They walked past the exhibit of native Illinois prairie wildlife and flowers. Then they walked by Sue; the largest T-Rex ever found had been reconstructed and cast a ferocious shadow on the half-lit walls.

Lloyd went down a stairway in the back of the building. Alexander followed him. "Where are we going?"

"To the maintenance area." Lloyd followed a twist of turns through narrow corridors until they finally reached one door that said "Engineers."

Fiddling with the keys, Lloyd finally found the right one and sprung the door open. Alexander followed him inside. The room was filled with steel boiler pipes. In one corner was a small drafting table with a clock and half-eaten ham sandwich. Next to it was a utility closet. "What are we doing back here?" Alexander asked.

"Deep tunnel," came Lloyd's reply.

Alexander thought about the deep tunnel. The vast sewer project had been started but never completed. It stretched for around 200 miles under the city's surface.

"We're connected and so is Soldier Field," Lloyd said as he grabbed flashlights and a large piece of paper with schematic drawings from the engineer's closet.

"How'd you find this place?" Alexander asked as he followed Lloyd to the back of the room. Lloyd bent down and opened a hatch. He turned and looked at Alexander.

"How can you ask that? I spend my life underground on digs in other countries—like I wouldn't find an underground tunnel in my backyard," Lloyd said.

"All right. All right." Alexander followed Lloyd down the narrow ladder. He stepped onto a platform and into darkness.

Lloyd switched on the flashlights. "Hold on. This thing is kind of rickety." He flipped a switch. With a lurch and a grind, the platform moved downward. It stopped with a loud thud. Alexander looked off into dark corridors. Unraveling the paper, Lloyd shone the light on it.

"We need to go that way." He pointed and they walked along the dark corridor. Alexander was almost afraid to switch on the light that Lloyd had given him. It shone into the red eyes of the rats, the only inhabitants of this cold, damp place. He could hear the water rushing around him.

"Don't worry. It's just like a cave." Lloyd shrugged off any concerns and kept leading the way.

The cave. Alexander pondered. Who knew when he started his research project that he would be spending so much time in caves? Luckily, he could rely on his guides—Lloyd here and Amat back in Sudan. He wondered how Amat was doing if things in Nairobi were as bad as here.

Alexander was glad he had walked so much in Africa because this walk seemed endless. They had walked down at least fifty feet of the main drain and they still hadn't hit the deep tunnel. It ranged from eighty feet to three hundred fifty feet, depending on what part of downtown Chicago you were in and how close to the river you were. It was built along the river to take the overflow from storm waters and sewage. After all, until the 1880s, Chicago had been underwater, literally.

When they finally reached the entrance to the deep tunnel, Alexander was amazed by its size. It was at least thirty-five feet across by thirty-five feet high.

"It's amazing. You can drive a truck through there," Alexander said.

"That was pretty much part of the plan, too," Lloyd said, pulling out his map again. "According to the map, it should be about a mile from the museum to Soldier Field."

They entered the tunnel and the rush of water became louder. Alexander longed for a coat as the chill struck him. As they walked, they could see the walls were decorated with graffiti gang signs and advertisements detailing what ladies would do for money.

"It's amazing," Alexander said, stopping to read one of the ads. "We all have the same drive."

"What do you mean?" Lloyd asked.

"Look around. No matter where we are, we need to show that we were there. Whether it's cave drawings in Africa or graffiti in Chicago or the painting of a church ceiling in Italy," Alexander said.

"Very interesting observation, Prof," Lloyd said.

"How do you know where you're going down here?" Alexander looked around at the mass of tunnels. "What if you're wrong?"

"Worse thing that happens is we end up in Macy's basement."

Alexander laughed.

They turned the corner and found an opening where the corridors split into six different directions. Lloyd checked his map, then looked up and pondered for a second which way to go. Finally he took the tunnel going to the far left. This tunnel opened into a large hub with another six tunnels branching off. They stopped abruptly. Alexander stepped back as Lloyd panned his flashlight along the side of the wall.

"What the hell is that?" Lloyd asked.

Alexander stared. Painted onto the side of the wall nearly 100 feet beneath the busy Chicago streets was a mural ripped from the pages of Revelation. It depicted the four horsemen riding through clouds. Lloyd walked over and ran his finger along the painting. Fresh paint stained his finger as he held it up to show Alexander. All four horsemen were wearing gray uniforms with blue patches.

Bears' Locker Room, Soldier Field

Rebekah looked around the room, wondering why this group had been singled out. She fingered the yellow wristband she had been tagged with. As far as she could see, she didn't have that much in common with Steven, the teen playing video games on his laptop, or the high school teacher. The Latinos who had confronted her on the truck and the others had been taken to a separate area. They had been tagged with white wristbands. From the window, she could see the others had been corralled onto the playing field, while this group was in the Bears' locker room.

After pacing around the room, Steven walked over and sat down next to her.

"Why do you think we're here and not out there?" Rebekah asked him.

Steven's answer was one word. "Computers."

"Huh?"

"We're all good with computers. I use them every day to conduct trades, that kid over there uses them to hack other systems, and I assume you are a programmer?"

"Yeah, but—"

Steven interrupted her, emphasizing his point. "Everyone in here seems to know computers." He pulled a pillbox out of his pocket. He popped a small pill that resembled an aspirin and then offered the box to her. "You want one?"

"What is it?" Rebekah asked, rubbing her aching head.

"Ecstasy," he whispered.

"No, thanks." Rebekah waved his hand and the pillbox away. She looked around the room again and noticed people were clustered together. She stood up. "I've got to find the ladies' room."

Steven stood up too. "I'll walk you down. It might not be safe out there."

She tried to shrug him off. "That's okay. I'll go by myself."

He refused to take no for an answer. They walked out of the room together and down the long corridor. The lights flickered on and off. She followed the yellow line that led from the locker room to the washroom. There were no guards walking the corridors. The entire first floor was sealed off from the rest of the stadium, so escape was not an issue. Steven walked by her side. "Rebekah, I don't know what's going to happen. I think we should stick together," Steven said.

"I appreciate the offer, but I'm kind of a loner. I can handle myself," she replied.

"Like you did on the truck."

"I would have handled it if you didn't step in."

"I think we might as well make the best of a bad situation." Steven turned and kissed her on the neck.

To get away, Rebekah backed up and ended up against the wall. "Hey, take it easy," she said.

He put his hands on both her sides, pinning her against the wall.

"I just fought off one guy. I don't need to go through this again," Rebekah said.

"What do you mean you fought off? Why do you think I saved you from that piece of garbage? I wanted you for myself." Steven kissed her, his lips sloppily covering her entire face.

Rebekah tried to scream, but Steven put his hand over her mouth. With his other hand, he reached down to undo the buttons on her blouse. She kneed him in the groin. When he backed off in pain, she ran down the hall blindly, stopping and trying door after door. At the first door that opened, she stumbled in. It was the men's bathroom. Through her sobs and her beating heart, she had been transported back years. She stepped into the furthest stall from the door and slammed it shut. She stood on top of the toilet so her shoes would not be seen.

"I don't want any ice cream. Don't stop," she repeated over and over even as the sobs coursed through her uncontrollably. She heard the clicking of heels outside the door. A scream rose up from her throat but turned into a gurgle. She heard the slow turning of the doorknob followed by the sound of shallow breathing.

He kicked in the first stall, then the second one. "I know you're here. If you scream, I'll kill you," he said in a low threatening voice.

As he kicked in the door where she was huddled, she thought she heard him say, "Becky, I brought you ice cream. Chocolate—your favorite."

A little nine year old inside her screamed "not this time." She took the door and rammed it into his face. He fell onto the floor, holding his nose. Rebekah took the heavy porcelain top off the toilet tank, hit him on the head, and then ran out the door.

Manager's Office, Soldier Field

John Stanley sat in the manager's office of Soldier Field viewing the list of curfew violators. He filtered through them until he came up with the group of computer programmers that he called forced volunteers, part of his newly formed Forced Volunteer Agency.

Mr. Stanley had been chosen to oversee the Forced Volunteer Agency based on his meticulous attention to detail as a CIA analyst. His uncompromising attitude had made him stand out. It had been four months since the military had first noticed a glitch in the NOMAD system, which controlled all US military operations. At first they thought it was a virus, then a hacker crashing into the system, but over the past four weeks the computers were degenerating at an increasing rate. It was the first computer system that was affected. The most sophisticated programs were hit first and the hardest. Others gradually were showing signs of damage, but not to this extent.

Using all their resources, Homeland Security, the FBI, and the CIA created a task force to stabilize the programs and keep them operational for nine hours at a time. Mr. Stanley had been selected to head the task force. The programs would degenerate and simply disappear. Bringing them back was another problem. Even using every government programmer and civilian forced volunteer, they could only keep the system going for nine hours at a time before needing to generate a new program.

Years ago, the CIA made a deal with the largest computer software manufacturers to install a backdoor chip into all of their programs that would allow the government to monitor all internet transactions, from porno downloads to international trade. But now they had to do things the old way, as Mr. Stanley called it, which involved culling through numerous paper files to find programmers, which in his case was more of a pleasure than a business. He was not reluctant to use any means necessary to convince people to do their duty for their country.

On his desk was a first edition of *Fahrenheit 451*. He appreciated the efficiency that the firemen used to cleanse the future society of non-conformists. Fire was an efficient way to cleanse, but it did leave behind soot and ashes. This was still too messy for Mr. Stanley's tastes. Whereas Bradbury's firemen used fire hoses surging with kerosene, Mr. Stanley would use a much more efficient method to cleanse the world.

As his perfectly manicured finger scanned the list of names, he came across one that seemed familiar but he couldn't place it. Rebekah Simmonds. It seemed he had heard that name before.

The door to his makeshift office opened, and an agent walked in. "Sir, we've had an incident," the agent said.

"What kind of incident?" Mr. Stanley set down his list and looked at his agent.

"One of the programmers is dead, and there's another one missing."

"What happened?"

"We went back to interview the programmers and two were missing. We figured they went to use the washroom. That's when we found the one, Steven Richards, dead on the floor. His head was bashed in."

"What about the other one?"

"We haven't been able to find her so far. Her name is Rebekah Simmonds."

"She can't have left the building. Search the grounds. Bring her to me," Mr. Stanley said. The agent walked out the door. Rebekah Simmonds was starting to be an issue. He did not like leaving things undone. He wanted to tidy up this Simmonds issue. Mr. Stanley returned to his list of forced volunteers, looking for any with potential. Next to each name was a short bio. A little star next to certain names marked those with special potential.

Under the Streets of Chicago

"This pipe will lead us right into the boiler room, according to my map," Lloyd said, folding the map up again and shoving it into his pocket. He and Alexander waded through the waste. As they had walked through the deep tunnel, it increasingly became a sea of sewage. At times, they had found themselves wading through waist-high pools. They reached a three-foot pipe and crawled through it. The pipe led up into a main drainage sewer. Together, the two were able to kick open the heavy metal grid sealing the pipe off. They finally found themselves standing in the bowels of the stadium. They were soaking wet and smelled like raw sewage. Plus, Alexander was freezing. Lloyd was exploring the engineer's desk.

"We made it this far. How do we find her?" Alexander asked.

"I'm sure they have a processing center to book everyone for holding. I would think they have separate quarters for women. We'll just have to find out where it is," Lloyd said.

"I guess we should just ask someone, huh?" Alexander replied.

"I got a better idea. Let's have her find us." Lloyd reached for the cell phone that was sitting on the desk. He punched some numbers into the phone and then hung up.

"What'd you do?"

"Gave her a code that should hopefully bring her right here. Can't take a chance calling; I'm sure they have tapped into any phones that are still working." Lloyd sat back, folding his hands behind his head. "Man, I'm tired."

***

Rebekah kept on running even though she knew Steven would never get up again. Even though it had been self-defense, she was afraid no one would believe her. She came to a dead stop when she felt a vibration against her hip. They had taken her purse, searched her for weapons, but they had missed her cell phone. She looked at it. The text lit up with "212***3*14." "What the?" she muttered to herself. "2-1-2-3-1-4."

She tried texting back, but the service was lost. She was not thinking clearly. It took her a minute to decipher the code. The signature 3.14 was the numeric formula for pi, which would mean Lloyd was texting her. She realized they must be looking for her and knew that she was inside the stadium, but they couldn't get to her. She might not have figured out the 212 if it hadn't been for the sign on the wall pointing to the boiler room. 212 degrees is the temperature at which water boils. She followed the sign. She hid in the shadows as two guards hurried down the hallway. After they disappeared, she opened the door slowly to the boiler room, not sure what to expect. Their stench hit her before she actually saw them.

In the dim light, Alexander made out her voluptuous curves. "Becky," Alexander whispered.

Closing the door, she walked into the office of the boiler room. Alexander and Lloyd stepped out of the shadows. She ran to Alexander and collapsed in his arms. "Get me out of here," she said as she clung to Alexander. After a few seconds, they followed Lloyd's secret route back to the Field Museum.

Lloyd shone his flashlight around the engineer's office. The room was dark, other than the weakening light of the flashlight. Lloyd tried to flick a switch. Nothing. "Damn, the power's out," he said. They stopped in Lloyd's office, washed up, and they changed into some of the spare clothes Lloyd kept in his office. Alexander wore Lloyd's Nintendo t-shirt and faded jeans that were too long for him.

They followed Lloyd's light down the hallway to the cafeteria. He scrounged around in the refrigerator. "Here, we can make sandwiches." Lloyd flung some lunchmeat at Rebekah and Alexander. They took the lunchmeat and some lukewarm sodas and headed down the corridor.

"I know where we can find some light and heat," Lloyd said. They ended up at the Neanderthal exhibit. The display depicted the discovery of fire, with early men dressed in fur sitting around a campfire with a saber-tooth tiger watching in the background. Lush greenery decorated the exhibit. "That fire runs off of natural gas. They wanted realism." Lloyd opened a valve and flicked his Bic. "Let there be light."

The campfire erupted in an orange glowing flame. Rebekah and Alexander took seats between their prehistoric brothers. Rebekah stared at one of the cavemen in the fire's light and looked at Lloyd and Alexander squatting and picking out lunchmeat. "It's funny how far we've come in a couple million years," she said with a sarcastic tone.

They both looked up with meat hanging out of their mouths.

"We'll camp here tonight. In the morning when the curfew's lifted, we'll head to my farm," Lloyd said.

"Won't there be soldiers and police?" Alexander asked.

"We'll keep to the back roads. I've avoided rush hour traffic for the past ten years. I know every side street, alley, and trail from here to Glencoe."

With that, they finished their dinner in silence. Alexander looked over at the cave. The amber of the fire danced off the cave's opening, floating to the top of the museum. It danced around and cast shadows over the walls. He thought about Amat.

After a restless night spent in the museum, Lloyd roused Rebekah and Alexander with some instant coffee that he boiled over the fire. He had found some Egg Beaters and scrambled those with strips of bologna. After they ate, they walked out into the predawn stillness. It was six a.m. and the sun was just casting a rosy glow over the lake. Seagulls were heading off the lake and scrounging around the parking lot, looking for half-eaten buns and popcorn.

They watched the sun rise over Lake Michigan. The Chicago skyline lit up from the rising sun was a beautiful sight. They walked to Lloyd's Pathfinder. Opening the compartment between the driver's and passenger's seats, Lloyd pulled out a nine millimeter. He stuck in a sixteen-round clip of hollow points, fed one into the chamber and placed it back into the compartment.

Rebekah watched him and then climbed into the back seat. "You think we're going to need that?"

"I've got this thing about unloaded guns. An unloaded one is more dangerous than a loaded one. I'd rather have no gun than have an unloaded gun sitting next to me," Lloyd said. "When they're unloaded, that's when you need it most."

"I forgot to tell you we were in Boy Scouts together. Always be prepared," Alexander told Rebekah with a chuckle. He sat in the passenger seat, buckling his seatbelt.

Lloyd turned on the truck and turned on the radio. Scanning through channels, all they heard were pre-recorded messages detailing the curfew ordinance. With a burst of static, an announcer came on with a live reading. "Good morning, Chicago. This is Brian Kirby, general manager for WSL AM 89. We've been instructed to turn our station over to the emergency broadcasting system. This is not a test. We want to thank you for all the years of listening to our station. Now here is Mr. Stanley from the emergency broadcasting system."

The voice changed into a high-pitched, almost effeminate voice. "The local curfew for Chicagoland is in effect from dusk until dawn until further notice. Police and fire emergency vehicles, along with hospitals and medical centers, will be open. We expect that utilities will be fully functional in a matter of hours, and we should be up and running soon. Schools and most businesses are closed. We have set a rations limit for groceries and other staples. Quantities will be limited per customer. We expect this to be a temporary situation, and we appreciate your cooperation. We're also in need of computer programmers to assist us with bringing the systems back on line. Lists have been posted in each city for paid volunteers to report to city hall for assignment. All businesses have been advised to cooperate and give employees a paid leave of absence. This will not affect your current job."

Inside Soldier Field Announcer's Booth

The camera and microphone shut off with a click. Mr. Stanley wiped his damp brow with a Kleenex; orange make-up covered the tissue. He was used to media spins; he figured it would be a week before the public knew the truth about how serious the situation was.

"Sir, we've searched all over the grounds. Ms. Simmonds is nowhere." His assistant came up to him after he ushered out the camera and radio crews.

"Get in touch with the police chief and local FBI. I want an all-points bulletin out on her. She's to be found and brought to me," Mr. Stanley ordered. "Are all the checkpoints in place leaving and entering the city?"

"Yes, sir."

"Then she has to be in the city somewhere. Find her." Mr. Stanley sat back in his chair. His assistant walked out.

He punched up the name Rebekah Simmonds on his computer. The screen flickered a few times and then a photo of Rebekah came up. He looked over the brief bio—her education and her background. He stopped when he saw the word Glasgow. It hit him where he had heard the name before. Professor McLean. She was listed as a contributor on the scientific papers McLean had published detailing the chaotic correlator program. Now he found that she was listed as a professor at the University of Chicago. He selected University of Chicago and ran a data search. About 230 names in the forced volunteer program appeared on the screen.

Out of those names, one appeared with two stars next to it. He pulled up the file for Kenny Maslow. Kenny was currently a supervisor of data input for streets and sanitation. As computers everywhere had started failing, the forced volunteer program had extended beyond the military. Mr. Stanley liked the fact that Kenny worked for streets and sanitation. Cleaning up garbage was a good thing. He made a phone call.

From the dark corner behind him, the squealing continued. At first it was a pleasant sound, but now it was annoying. The rat problem was getting worse. Mr. Stanley wondered if the rats knew the ship was sinking. He walked over to the corner of his office to the rattrap he had set earlier. The rat was gnawing at his leg trying to break free. It reminded Mr. Stanley of his childhood. He bent down to look closer. "Filthy little beasts," he said, picking up the trap. The rat dangled, gnawing and squealing. Mr. Stanley took out his Zippo lighter.

Lake Shore Drive, Chicago

Lloyd turned onto Lake Shore Drive. Chicago was waking up. As he drove along the side streets, they could see people leaving their homes. Lines were forming at the local grocery and drug stores. Traffic on the main highway was shut down; the city was literally closed off. Winding his way through the side streets that ran along Sheridan Road and the city's lakefront, they realized the devastation of one night of panic. The scene hinted at *Les Miserables*. The affluent homes on the lakefront were vandalized and scarred with graffiti. Mailboxes were uprooted from the curb. Lawn ornaments lay on their sides and windows were cracked. It didn't take much to bring out the hatred for the rich. The large homes of the upper class were just a few feet from the projects, which had been built on high-priced lakefront property. Over the past few years, a re-gentrification program had been started. The projects were being forced out by million-dollar townhouses. Every day, the poor looked out their windows at the new townhouses, wondering if their building would be the next to be demolished.

As they entered the first suburb leaving Chicago, military vehicles blocked off Sheridan Road. Cars leaving the city were being stopped. IDs were checked. They watched as some people were pulled from their vehicles and lined up on the side of the road.

"What are we going to do?" Rebekah asked, looking around nervously at the soldiers wielding their M-16s.

"I think this is where we get out." Lloyd pulled the Pathfinder to the side of the road. They were still about twenty cars from the checkpoint. He grabbed his backpack and put the gun in it. They got out of the car and walked through the campus of Northwestern University. Although classes were canceled, there were still maintenance people and a few students aimlessly wandering around the campus.

They left the campus and walked through the surrounding backyards and side streets, avoiding the main roads, the military, and the police. After a few hours, they reached the forest preserve, which was accessed by a single lane blacktop road. The Cook County Forest Preserve encompassed miles of woods and lakes along Chicago's north shore. It was bordered by exclusive, expensive homes. This narrow road led to one of the preserves that was backed by mansions. "It's not much farther," Lloyd said.

They trudged slowly through the forest preserve before seeing a lone iron gate that stood at the end of the blacktopped road. "Here we are." Lloyd walked up to the gate.

"How are we going to get in?" Rebekah asked.

"Watch," Alexander said.

Lloyd opened a hidden panel and punched in a code. The gate swung open. Rebekah followed Lloyd and Alexander through the gate. Lloyd closed the gate behind him. She stood and stared at the extensive grounds, which resembled a nineteenth-century British country estate.

"You call this a farm. It looks like the Prince of Wales lives here," Rebekah said as they walked the half-mile drive.

Lloyd laughed. "We call this a cottage." The red-bricked driveway was lined with fifty-foot poplar trees. The cottage was a French provincial three-story brick house that loomed out over the driveway and was reflected in the lake immediately to the right of the drive.

"You call that a cottage?" Rebekah repeated.

Lloyd shrugged. As they walked, three tailless dogs came running from over by the lake. They were barking. "Don't be afraid," Lloyd told her. The dogs jumped and somersaulted around him, licking his face and pushing each other out of the way to get near him.

"What kind are they?" Rebekah asked, stepping carefully to avoid their exuberance.

"Australian shepherds. They're out of control," Alexander said, standing next to her.

"No, they're not. They just have an excess of energy," Lloyd said, leading the way to the house. The dogs circled around him. He threw a ball onto the lawn. Barking loudly, the three dogs ran after it. "The black tricolor is Rocky, the red tricolor is Bandit, and the blue merle one is Bear. Bandit's their mom. She keeps them in line."

Rebekah and Alexander watched as the dogs bounced all over Lloyd, kissing him and wagging their tailless butts. The Aussie has the heart of a lion and endless energy. They were bred to work all day.

After the enthusiasm died out, they followed him into the large house. "This place is huge," Rebekah said, looking around.

Lloyd looked around for the housekeeper or a gardener. It seemed everybody was gone.

The palladium stained glass window flooded the three-story foyer with morning sunlight. The foyer opened into the hallway, which had a marble stairway, mahogany trim, and a crystal chandelier. A large picture of Lloyd with Sue the T-Rex, was framed in the hallway.

"She's a beauty, isn't she?" Lloyd asked, pointing to the picture. "Just imagine what it was like back then. That's why I get such a kick out of archeology. It's like having my own private time machine. I can turn time back and imagine walking the earth with her. It's an incredible feeling." Lloyd led the way to the kitchen. "I only keep this place so the dogs have a chance to run. I actually have a one-bedroom apartment near Lincoln Park."

They entered the kitchen. Lloyd flipped on a small television. The news was on and an announcer was talking at a rapid pace. "The death toll stands at twenty-five, and more than 1,000 people have been arrested. If you don't have to leave your house, don't. Chicago police are arresting on sight anyone walking on the streets after curfew. The county jail is full. A temporary holding cell has been set up at Soldier Field."

Alexander walked back into the room. "This is turning into Nazi Germany. What happened to our rights?" He popped open a can of Coke and passed one to Rebekah.

"The minute they declared martial law we lost our rights. We are now officially in a police state," she replied.

"I want to show you guys something. Follow me," Lloyd said, leading his way down a back staircase.

Rebekah looked at the hidden passageway that Lloyd had led them to. "This is so medieval," she said.

"Come on down to the dungeon." They followed Lloyd down a steel staircase. Alexander had flashbacks to the cave and wondered if Amat had found anything yet. He pictured those brave souls and wondered what they thought as they descended into their final resting place. A chill ran up his spine. Fluorescent bulbs lit the hallway. Lloyd punched in a code on a pad next to the steel door and the door swung open.

"This is my doomsday, zombie apocalypse room. Ironic, isn't it?" Lloyd asked, walking in.

"I always thought you were a little off," Alexander said, following him in. Every weapon known to man was on a shelf in the room. There were machine guns, handguns, and missiles. There was also a supply of canned food and bottled water. "Check this out. It's a stinger—ground-to-air rocket launcher. I can take out a 747 with it," Lloyd said, picking up one weapon and waving it around.

"Now you're scaring me," Rebekah said.

"My dad, who worked with Alex's dad, was a survivalist. He was a Navy SEAL and always believed in being prepared. That's where I get it from."

Rebekah looked at Alexander, who just shrugged his shoulders.

Lloyd threw Alexander a duffel bag. "What's this for?" Alexander asked.

"It's my Omega man care package." Lloyd scanned the walls. He picked and chose things and threw them into a large duffle bag. "We might have to leave at a moment's notice. We have to be prepared," Lloyd said.

"You really think it's going to get that bad?" Rebekah asked.

"Well, it's not going to get any better."

Lloyd put in a collection of arms, food, and a black metal box. "What's that?" Alexander asked.

"A state-of-the-art satellite phone. Once the landlines and cell phones are down, this will be our last contact with civilization. That's if there's any civilization left to contact."

"Speaking of which, I need to use your phone. I need to get in touch with Amat," Alexander said, lugging the duffel bag up the stairs.

Back in the kitchen, Alexander picked up the handset on the wall and heard a fast busy signal. Picking up the bag containing the satellite phone, he dialed the University of Nairobi and got the archeology department's secretary. "I'm looking for Amat Smeher."

"We haven't seen him. He's not in his office," the secretary said in English.

"May I leave a message for him?" Alexander asked.

"Yes, I will leave it on his desk."

Alexander left Lloyd's satellite phone number.

University of Nairobi, Kenya

Amat stood outside the laboratory at the University of Nairobi. He was waiting for the results of the carbon dating of bones and remnants he had brought back from the cave. Normally a patient man, Amat had lost his patience and kept checking his analog watch. His fancy new digital watch had stopped working a few weeks before. All digital clocks at the university had seemed to stop working. It would be dark soon, and no one was allowed on the streets after dark. He did not want to risk being picked up by the police, but he refused to leave until he had the test results. Besides, the streets of Nairobi were not a place to be after dark under normal circumstances.

Moses Khanu, Amat's longtime friend, had rushed the results for him. Now Moses came out of the lab.

"What do we have?" Amat asked, ignoring the customary exchange of greetings.

"The skeletal remains are 6,000 years old," Moses said.

Amat didn't say anything.

Moses handed Amat a sheet of paper. "This might help you with answers. We were able to decipher the first scroll. I need to get back. See you, my friend."

Amat watched Moses walk away. He slowly walked back to his office. He saw the message that Alexander had called. He would try to return the call even though curfew was closing in. He tried three times but could not get an outside line. Nairobi phone lines were not very reliable. He would try once again when he got home and shoved the paper with Alexander's numbers inside his pocket.

Amat walked out of the university and headed home. He had left his car at home, wanting to avoid the crazy traffic. There were gangs of homeless teenage children on the street; he quickened his pace, almost running. He heard the shrill scream of sirens and then local police and guards wielding machine guns surrounded the streets. People were hurrying to get behind the safety of closed doors. The sight of machine gun police was not new to Amat, but the numbers were. It scared him so he quickened his pace. As he turned the corner to his street, he faced a mob of rioters. Police with tear gas filled the street as the soldiers clubbed the rioters, driving them into trucks. Then there was an explosion inside Amat's head and he was out.

Chicago's North Shore

Lloyd stood up from the couch, stretching. "I'm going to bed. There's six bedrooms upstairs. There are clean sheets in the hall closet. Help yourselves to whatever you need."

"One of his bedrooms is bigger than my whole apartment," Alexander whispered to Rebekah. They were sitting side by side on the black leather couch. He stood up to put out the fire.

"Leave it. I'm enjoying it." Rebekah leaned back on the couch.

Lloyd headed up the stairs, the three dogs following him.

"I love sitting in front of the fire. One of the nice things about my flat in Glasgow was having a fireplace and needing to use it."

"Tell me about Scotland," Alexander said, sitting back down next to her. He refilled both of their wine glasses.

"I used to sit for hours and talk with Angus about life and death."

Alexander cleared his throat. "Angus? Is he...was he...your boyfriend?"

"Maybe fifty years ago he might have been. Actually he was my mentor. He was the reason I decided to go to the University of Glasgow. After that, I fell in love with Scotland for its own sake. And I made other friends. We played Scrabble for hours and talked around the fire. Tell me more about Africa."

Alexander talked for a while and moved in closer. "What about your family, friends? Do you need to call someone?"

A look of sadness crossed Rebekah's face. "My foster parents and I didn't really get along. No brothers, no sisters. How about you? No one waiting for you?"

"My mom died when I was young. My dad is chief requisitions officer for the armed forces in Washington," Alexander said. "I spoke to him when I first got back from Africa. I tried to call him today, but the lines were busy. I'll try again tomorrow."

"Were you able to get through to anyone else? I haven't heard a phone ring all day."

"The phones have been spotty since this afternoon." They both sat quietly and stared at the fire. Seeing Alexander's face silhouetted by the fire and the love in his eyes when he talked about his dad drew her closer to him. She hadn't thought about him in that way. At least until now. She had never had much luck with men because most men weren't able to handle her combination of beauty and brains. But Alexander seemed comfortable with her. As she pondered the possibilities, Alexander turned and kissed her on her lips. It was a quick kiss. She almost thought she imagined it. "I've been wanting to do that since I first saw you," he said.

She came out of her trance and looked confused.

Alexander sat back. "I'm sorry. I shouldn't have done that."

"You took me by surprise. It's okay." Rebekah reached over and wrapped her arms around him.

Nairobi Jail

"I have to get out. I have to make a phone call," Amat said as he stood grasping the bars, looking out into the empty hallway. "Guard, guard."

"My brother, we'll never get out," a voice said from behind him. "All the guards have gone home."

Amat turned to see a distinguished-looking African in his sixties with an elegant air. "My name is Amat Smeher."

"Hello, I am Dr. Oleg Cham." The two men shook hands.

"What are you doing here?" Amat asked.

"What are we all doing here?" The doctor threw his hands up in the air. "My daughter and I were on our way home from the hospital. There were rioters in the streets. The police were trying to break it up. Some people got hurt. I stopped to help and got caught up in the mob. Thank God, my daughter got away. She will find me," he said with a calm confidence.

The two men sat on the cold, damp floor next to each other. To pass the time, Amat told the doctor the story of the cave.

"I like your watch." A tall native with dreadlocks sat down between the doctor and Amat. He stared at the doctor's watch.

The doctor took his hand and covered his wrist.

"I'd sure like a watch like that," the man repeated, eyeing the doctor's wrist.

Another native came over and towered behind Amat.

"This gentleman's a doctor. Leave him alone," Amat said.

The first man reached for the doctor's wrist. Amat grabbed his hand and pinned him against the wall. Amat was wiry but very strong from years of battling in the jungle. With one punch, the man was knocked out cold. The other native blindsided Amat and knocked him to the ground. He kicked him in the ribs and head. Before Amat passed out, he saw the doctor take a chair and hit it over his assailant's head.

When he came to, there was a beautiful young Nubian woman standing by his bedside. It took a while to adjust his vision. It faded in and out. "Papa, he's waking up," the girl called.

"Where am I?" Amat said, trying to sit up. His head felt thirty pounds heavier than it usually did. Explosions of pain surged through him as he gently eased back down on the pillows.

"Don't get up. You're not ready. You're in my papa's house. I am Ariet," she said, pushing him back down.

Amat, through his blurred vision, could see her young beauty. He tried to crack a smile.

"Well, my friend, we had quite an adventure last night, didn't we?" The doctor came in and took his wrist, looking for his pulse.

"Last night?" Amat rubbed his head.

"That's right. You've been asleep for the last twelve hours. If Ariet hadn't rescued me, I'm afraid you would have slept forever. You were bleeding quite profusely."

"I need to make a phone call." Amat sat up again. This time was easier. He looked around the room. Rich mahogany and teak woodwork scrolled along the walls. The furniture was fashioned from heavy wood and looked extremely old.

"I'm sorry, but the phones are down. I've been trying to call the hospital since last night."

"I must get to the university. There's a satellite phone there—perhaps it's working."

"I really don't think you should move for a couple days."

"This is important. I need to call the States." Amat sat on the edge of the bed.

"Nothing is that important," Ariet said. She poured him a glass of orange drink.

Amat downed it in one gulp. "This is. I must call my friend in America."

"But, Amat, my friend, the university is on the other side of Nairobi. It's at least twenty minutes by car and these roads are not the best under good conditions."

"I need to try."

"I'll go with you," the doctor said.

"No, Papa," Ariet said.

"Don't worry. I'll protect your father."

"Oh, like you protected him in prison."

"Ariet, hush." Her father held out a hand to silence her.

"No, Papa. If you idiots insist on going, I will go with you."

"What can you do?"

"Drive the car and bring my pistol."

Amat admired her courage. "Let us go then."

"She's right. You're in no condition to drive and my eyes are bad. We need her," the doctor said.

Chicago's North Shore

Rebekah and Alexander lay in front of the dwindling fire. The amber light made Rebekah's hair crackle with a brilliant gleam. "Do you ever wonder what it would be like to be the last people on earth?" Alexander asked.

"You're way past needing a line with me," Rebekah said, giggling.

Alexander ran his hands through her hair. The moment was interrupted by a distant ringing. "Do you hear something?" Rebekah asked.

"I think it's the phone. It could be Amat." He jumped up and ran to the kitchen. "Hello," he said as he grabbed the receiver.

"Alexander, my friend," Amat said as the phone crackled and hissed.

"Amat, is that you?" Alexander practically screamed to be heard.

"Yes, I have much news to tell you." The phone lines cracked in and out.

"Are you safe? How are things in Nairobi?"

"It's very dangerous. How are things in Chicago?"

"We're safe for now, but I don't know for how long."

"I got the results back from the carbon dating."

"And?" Alexander asked, holding his breath.

"The bones date back 6,000 years."

"Amat, I'm losing you. Did you say 6,000?"

"Yes, 6,000. There is more," Amat shouted into the phone as the static grew louder. "We deciphered the first page of the scroll."

"What does it say?"

Amat read, "'We can no longer exist together. Brother is turning against brother. We are finding refuge in this safe place. I am writing this in case we never leave this place. We find it impossible to communicate to each other. Our father's language has been lost in our quest for power. We have forgotten the old ways and I fear this is the end.'"

"I've got to come there. Is there more?" Alexander asked. He heard silence. "Amat? Amat!" he called to no avail. The phone was dead.

University of Nairobi, Kenya

Amat sat in the administration office of the natural history department at the University of Nairobi. After dialing and receiving a busy tone, he hung up the phone and tried to redial Alexander. "There's no dial tone," he said to the doctor. They heard a crash and the window behind them shattered.

"We must go. It's not safe here," Oleg said. "We must go back to my house."

Amat gathered the satellite phone and the scrolls and followed Oleg back to the Range Rover. Ariet was waiting for them. "I can drive now," Amat told her, motioning her to move over.

"What's wrong with my driving?"

"We have to get back to your place and get there fast."

She crawled over the stick shift. Amat and Oleg climbed in. Amat took off. People crowded the streets, and some cars were abandoned and on fire. There was gunfire and rock throwing. There were many broken windows. People were looting stores, taking anything they could carry. By the time they reached the doctor's house, Amat's fears had been realized. The gates to the driveway were hanging off the hinges. He stopped the car in the drive, and they looked at the scene in front of them. A portion of the house was burning; looters were helping themselves to furniture and anything else they could carry.

Ariet cried, "My home. My beautiful home." It was Ariet's childhood home. Her mother had died when she was young, and Ariet had taken over the care of the house. She kept everything in perfect order. She loved that home. She opened the car door and ran towards the hordes of looters.

Amat ran after her. "Ariet, stop," he called. In the frenzy, people pushed and shoved her to the ground. After fighting his way through the crowd, Amat scooped her off the ground and beat his way back to the car. He placed her on her father's lap in the back seat. He took off at a rapid pace as people banged on the car.

"My dear, Ariet," Oleg said as he cradled her forehead. "These are just things."

"Papa, my home."

"It's just a house. The important thing is we're together."

Amat turned around to look at them in the backseat. "We have to leave the city."

Oleg just nodded his head as he cradled his daughter. "Where are we going to go?"

"I know a safe place. I've spent more of my time in the jungle than in the city. I prefer the dangers of the brush to the dangers of my brothers."

Chicago's North Shore

Wearing flannel pajama bottoms, Lloyd came down the stairs. He flipped on the television. A newscaster was reading. "Welcome to the all-news universe," Lloyd said, opening the door to let the dogs out.

"Shush, I want to hear this," Rebekah said.

The television flickered. Its image wavered and then reappeared. "This is a special report. The United Arab Nations have joined together in an attack against Israel. Israel has asked for help from the UN. Our troops in the Persian Gulf are being asked to monitor the situation. We will keep you informed."

"I bet my dad is going nuts." Alexander picked up the phone again. He tried to dial unsuccessfully. While trying, he filled Lloyd in on Amat's phone call.

"We have to get over there," Lloyd said, breaking some eggs into a bowl.

Rebekah took the phone from Alexander's hand. "Who are you calling?" Alexander asked.

"The airlines."

Lloyd laughed. "You missed part of the newscast. No foreign travel. The airlines are shut down. All that is flying are military aircraft."

"I'm going to try my dad again," Alexander took the phone back. After about ten tries, he finally got through. "Dad."

"Alex, I've been trying to get you. I've tried you everywhere. Are you safe?" His father's voice boomed over the phone.

"I'm at Lloyd's house. In the brick-walled fortress."

"I'm going to send a plane for you. You'll be safer here in Washington with me."

"Dad, I need to get to Africa."

"Son, you can't go there. We're putting out fires all over, and especially in Africa."

"But we're on the brink of changing history."

"So am I, son, so am I. History is changing all around."

"Can you get us a plane to Africa? I'll tell you now that if you can't do it, we'll find a way."

"Come to Washington and we'll talk about it. I'll send an escort to Lloyd's to make sure you get to the airport. Look, son, I'll see you when you get here. I have to go," Colonel Talcott said, rushing off the phone as someone walked into his office, waving papers.

Alexander hung up the phone and turned to his two waiting friends. "I didn't get us to Africa, but we're a little closer. My dad is getting us seats on a troop courier plane that stops in Washington. We'll work on him once we get there. He's sending someone to pick us up at first light."

The next morning, the black military suburban showed up promptly at 0500. Taking just what they could carry, and the dogs after a brief argument, they crowded into the back of the vehicle and watched the miles fly by the window. There was an eerie stillness even for five a.m. Not a single car could be seen for miles. When they hit the main hub of the highway, it was still barren except for the occasional military vehicle. When they reached the checkpoint at O'Hare International Airport, they were relieved to find Alexander's name on the guard's list. After thanking their escort, Alexander went to talk to the commander while Lloyd and Rebekah watched the action around them. The dogs sat patiently next to Lloyd.

"Your dad called me," the commander said, waving a cigar. "I got you on a C7 leaving in an hour. Leave your gear over there." He pointed by the door. "Your dad didn't mention the dogs."

"I can't go without them," Alexander said. "They have been specially trained."

"I doubt that. You can take them, but they have to be caged," the commander said.

Alexander went to the vacant baggage claim area and found three unclaimed crates. Lloyd and he secured the dogs in the crates and watched them loaded onto the plane.

Washington, DC

Upon arriving at Dulles, they found a car waiting for them. Alexander drove them to his dad's house. When they arrived at his father's Georgetown brownstone, Alexander cooked steaks on the grill while Lloyd threw a ball in the backyard with his dogs. Rebekah sat on a lawn chair eyeing the setting sun, thinking how normal everything seemed.

Alexander's father arrived home. He gave his son a big hug. "Well, son, I'm not going to lie to you. It doesn't look good. The Pentagon's computers have whatever virus is affecting the rest of the systems. Our IT specialists keep putting Band-Aids on the problems that crop up. If one of those breaks, it will be gone. All communications are down except for some backup satellites. We thought at first it was a hacker, then a terrorist attack. But it's much bigger than that. War is breaking out all over the world. Peaceful countries have turned on their neighbors. Brother against brother."

Alexander stopped and found it hard to swallow the words "brother against brother." He felt himself get dizzy and hung onto the side of a lawn chair to steady himself.

"What's wrong?" his dad asked, offering him a beer.

Taking a large swig, Alexander filled his dad in on the scroll.

"How does that fit in with what's going on now?" his dad asked.

"I don't know. That's why I have to go there. We're talking about a piece of history that changes everything we know about mankind."

"I can get you on a troop plane, but I can't guarantee your safety. Son, I don't like it; you're all I have, and I don't want to lose you. But if you feel that strongly about it, I'm not going to keep you because I couldn't if I wanted to. You're stubborn like your mom. There was no arguing with her either once her mind was set on something. I can get you a flight out tomorrow to Egypt and pack you with any supplies you need."

"I don't need anything, Dad. Lloyd packed a bag."

It was almost one a.m. Lloyd was asleep in an overstuffed chair surrounded by his three dogs. Lloyd never thought of them as his. The Aussie was one of the smartest breeds, often outsmarting their owners. Lloyd felt part of the pack with them rather than a master.

***

Colonel Talcott took out three brandy snifters from behind a china cabinet and placed them on the coffee table in front of the fireplace. Without speaking a word, he went up the stairs of the historic two-story brownstone. Alexander looked around at all the family antiques. Some of them his mother had brought with her from Ireland. His father hadn't changed the house since his mother had died. When he was young, he could remember sitting in her arms in front of the fireplace reading Curious George books. He used to love to snuggle with her while they waited for his dad to come home from work. When his dad would come home, her eyes would light up. They would all gather into a bear hug before sitting down at the large mahogany table for dinner.

His parents met while serving in Vietnam. His mother was a nurse in a MASH unit and his dad was on night patrol when he was shot in the leg by a sniper. It had been desk duty for him since then. She tended both his wounds and his heart. A year later, Alexander was born.

When Alexander turned ten, things changed. His dad was gone for months at time, and his mom seemed tired all the time. As he grew stronger, his mother seemed to weaken. One morning he woke up to find his mother gone, and his aunt sitting in the living room crying. His father burst open the door and held Alexander tightly. "Come with me now."

They drove to the hospital. "What's wrong? What's wrong?" Alexander asked repeatedly as his father drove the Dodge Diplomat silently. He knew something was wrong. When he approached the entrance to St. Anne's Hospital, he cried uncontrollably. His dad stopped the car, turned around and said, "You have to stop crying. You don't want your mother seeing how upset you are. You have to be brave, you understand?"

Wiping the tears from his eyes, Alexander nodded, wanting to ask why. When they entered the ICU, his mother was on an oxygen mask. She managed to smile through the mask and wave to him. Alexander forced a smile and took her hand. Alexander's father kissed her forehead. A white-coated doctor came in and pulled his father out of the room. Alexander sat down next to his mother. She pulled the oxygen mask off. "Alexander, I don't want you to be scared," she said. "I'm sick but the doctors are going to make me better. Tomorrow I'm having surgery to take out what's making me sick."

"Mom, what's wrong with you? "

"I have cancer. But it's all going to be okay. God will watch over all of us. I want you to listen to your father and your aunt. And I want you to pray for me. Will you do that for me?"

"Yes, Mom, I will pray hard. I will pray very hard every day."

The next day Mrs. Talcott had both her breasts removed. For the next year, she underwent radiation and chemotherapy treatments. Each time she seemed to be in remission but the cancer would come back. She wound up back in the hospital with Father Paul at her side, praying over her and reading from the Bible. Alexander would kneel next to the bed and pray as hard as he could each time.

After all treatment options were exhausted, his mother came home to rest. Alexander's father made her comfortable in her bedroom so she could see her rose garden out her window and smell the peonies in bloom.

Father Paul came everyday. Alexander continued his prayers. Finally he asked Father Paul, "Why isn't God listening?"

"God hears our prayer, but he answers them in his own way," Father Paul answered. "His will be done."

Alexander didn't like that answer. He had done everything right. He followed all the rules. He prayed, read his Bible, went to church, lit candles. He even did all his chores around the house without being asked. Why wasn't God listening?

One day, Alexander came home from school to find the driveway lined with cars. Some he recognized, some he didn't. Dropping his backpack, he ran into the house. Father Paul was performing the sign of the cross as he raised the white sheet over his mother's face. His father stood nearby. The toughest man Alexander knew was in tears, hanging onto the bed so as not to fall. Alexander took in that moment and would relive it the rest of his life. Always the same question: "Why? Why wasn't God listening? Why couldn't God hear me?" Alexander never prayed again.

***

Alexander's father came down the stairs carrying a dusty bottle. "I've been saving this, son, for your wedding day."

Everyone was silent. He poured them all two fingers of brandy. Alexander swirled around the amber liquid, realizing this might be the last drink he would ever share with his dad. While Alexander sat around the fire glow exchanging stories with his dad, Rebekah went into the kitchen to call Scotland.

The phone systems had been spotty in the last two weeks, so it took several attempts to get through, but Rebekah finally reached the main administration office at the university. "This is Rebekah Simmonds. I'm a colleague of Professor McLean's. I haven't been able to reach him at his flat. I was wondering if you might know how to reach him."

There was dead silence for a moment. She thought she had lost the connection. With a heavy Scottish brogue, the voice on the other side said, pausing over each word, "Ma'am, I'm so sorry. You haven't heard. Oh, I'm so sorry. I don't know how to tell you this, but the professor is dead."

"Dead? How can that be?" Rebekah asked, sinking down onto the bar stool by the kitchen counter.

"They pulled him and his car out of Glenlick Lake late early yesterday morning. Apparently he had been driving home from the pub and had fallen asleep."

"That's not possible. That's not possible." Rebekah shook her head.

"Lassie, I'm so sorry, but I'm afraid it's true." And then the phone went dead.

Rebekah walked back into the living room. "What's wrong?" Alexander asked.

"Professor McLean. He's dead." She sat onto the couch next to Alexander, who put his arm around her shoulder. "They said he fell asleep while driving drunk, but it's not possible."

"It happens. You said he was a heavy drinker."

"Not with Angus." Rebekah shook her head. "First of all, he could drink ten men under the table and not fall asleep. Secondly, if he was that drunk, he would walk the 100 yards to his flat on campus. And thirdly, since his eyesight went bad, he hasn't driven in ten years," Rebekah said.

"Are you saying he was killed?" Lloyd asked, waking up from his sleep.

"I know Angus. He wouldn't have died like this, and if he was attacked he would have fought like hell. I have to go find out what happened. I have to go to Glasgow."

"Becky, I'm sorry and understand how you feel. It's too dangerous. We have to make it to Egypt," Alexander said.

"You don't understand. It's not just about Angus. Everything I have, including the correlation program, is just a first-generation program. He has the masters. I have to get to them before they do."

"Who's they?" Alexander asked.

"The ones that locked me up in the stadium; the ones that killed Angus," Rebekah said.

"Why were you locked up?" Colonel Talcott said.

"We got caught up in a riot downtown, and the military police brought me to Soldier Field. They were wearing blue patches, not US," Rebekah said.

"NATO has been helping our military police in some of the larger cities," Colonel Talcott said.

"Don't you find that kind of strange, Colonel Talcott, that NATO would be deployed on US soil?" Lloyd said, petting Bandit's fur.

"There's a lot of unusual deployment lately. Our military is spread thin throughout the world."

"When I was in the containment center, I heard they were separating everyone with computer programming experience. I think that's why they pulled me in, because of the correlator program I worked on with Professor McLean. Now he's dead," Rebekah said.

"The president has established a program called Forced Volunteers or FVAs," Colonel Talcott said. "Nobody says that name. The program identifies assets who can help keep our computer systems running."

"How bad is it, Colonel?" Lloyd said.

"We've not been able to identify the virus. We've only been able to keep essential systems up and running nine hours at a time before they crash. No one understands the countdown clock yet, but it seems to be running down. After each new reboot, eventually I think we won't be able to bring systems online at all." The colonel paused. "At first, we contacted the major players—Microsoft, Google, Apple—and we borrowed their key staff under a temporary leave of absence. With the FVA, we stopped asking and started taking."

"Jesus, it's all coming true," Lloyd said.

"I need to get to Scotland," Rebekah said. "Whoever killed Professor McLean is not going to stop until they have the correlation program. It doesn't matter where I am."

"We have a transport leaving for London tomorrow. I can get you on there and you can get to Scotland from London. From London we have supplies going to Egypt three days after that. If you miss the flight out of London, you're stuck there for a month until the next shipment," Colonel Talcott said, leaning back in his leather armchair.

"That's all we need—three days." Rebekah replied.

In the morning, the colonel stopped at the base health clinic so Rebekah could get shots for their journey. Lloyd and Alexander were up to date on theirs. Lloyd had gone on ahead to the airstrip to see if he could make room for the dogs on the plane.

He was standing on the runway, talking to the staff sergeant, who was overseeing the loading of the plane. "What would it take to get my three dogs on the plane?" Lloyd asked, pointing to his dogs who were sitting quietly underneath a shade tree.

"An act of Congress," the sergeant said as he reached for his ringing cellular phone.

Lloyd pulled out his wallet. "Instead of a bunch of senators, how about a bunch of presidents?" He handed him $10,000.

"Not only will that get them on the plane, but it will get them in first class. I'll even serve the drinks," the sergeant said, taking the money.

Lloyd watched a little later as his beloved pets were loaded onto the passenger side of the plane. He would be able to sit with them. Life was good. Alexander walked up to him. "I see you took care of that."

"Things haven't changed. Money still talks," Lloyd said.

"I'll call in some favors and have a helicopter drop you in Glasgow," Colonel Talcott said, walking up to them.

"Thanks, Dad," Alexander said.

"Thanks, Colonel Talcott," Rebekah said.

"Now remember, you have to be to Heathrow in three days to catch the flight to Egypt, where our base is. There'll be a car waiting for you. You'll also have a local escort. They will only be able to take you as far as the Sudan border. Fighting has escalated between the Muslims and Christians. It's a real holy war," the colonel said.

Rebekah listened, fondling the gold cross around her neck.

"I'd keep that hidden if I were you, especially if you go through northern Sudan," the Colonel told her.

"Colonel, we're ready to go," the pilot said, stepping over for a moment. He saluted the colonel, who returned the salute. He then walked up to the plane.

"Well, bye, son." The colonel looked at Alexander.

"Bye, Dad." Alexander held out his hand. "Thanks for everything." They shook hands, looked at each other for a long moment, and then wrapped their arms around each other in a bear hug.

Alexander followed Rebekah onto the plane. He waved to his dad before the hatch closed behind them. The colonel stood on the tarmac watching until the plane took off, wondering if it was the last time he would see his son.

Nairobi, Kenya

"We just need to get to Loki," Amat said to the guard as he stopped the Range Rover at a checkpoint on the outer border of Nairobi.

"Do you have a pass?" the guard asked, shining a light on their faces. Ariet was sleeping, her head leaning on the doctor's shoulder.

"No, sir, we do not," Oleg said, leaning forward. Ariet stirred.

"I'm sorry, no vehicles are allowed on the road without a pass."

"What do we do now?" Amat asked, knowing they couldn't go back.

The doctor took his watch off and handed it to Amat, who shook his head. "Give it to him. It's already caused us enough trouble," Oleg said.

Amat handed the guard the watch. The guard studied it for a minute, and then waved them forward. Amat steered the utility vehicle through the outer streets. The roads were bumpy and full of holes. Parts were asphalt, but some of the asphalt had worn away and given in to dirt and dust.

The Range Rover bounced along the road. Every so often, Amat would have to put on the brakes and swerve to avoid the huge holes. His arm and leg ached from downshifting. A soft rain pelted the windshield. They passed by the Kenya National Animal Preserve. Normally there would be hordes of tourists waiting to drive into the park, but now he could only glimpse an occasional rhino through the trees. Many people were walking along the side of the road. The women were carrying baskets on their heads. In some ways, the events of the last few days hadn't changed the African landscape. For these people, life continued.

"Ariet's asleep again. I gave her something to calm her down. Where are we going?" Oleg asked.

"If we can make it through the cities, I will take you to my homeland. There's a village far removed from this madness. There's no police, no soldiers, no guns. If we can make it before the heavy rains, we'll be safe there," Amat said, staring straight ahead.

"Then what?"

"Then we'll see," Amat said, speaking with a calm assuredness he didn't quite feel. He hadn't really had any time to think. He only knew something was driving him back to the cave.

London

The troop transport to Heathrow was a quiet flight. Rebekah dozed with her head against Alexander's shoulder. The three had been surrounded by a troop of marines decked out in the standard sand-covered camo used in Desert Storm. This troop's next stop would be Egypt. Some of them had fought in the Gulf War, but Lloyd observed their mood was different this time.

"It's more of a war than a police action," he explained to Alexander after talking to some of the soldiers.

"How do you mean?" Alexander asked.

"I can't explain it, but these guys were telling me about their experience in the Gulf and their thoughts about this." Lloyd plopped down in his seat next to Alexander. "The Gulf had limited troops on the ground. Everything was calculated according to the minimum needed to accomplish the mission. This is all-out warfare. They're all wearing individual dosimeters, IDMs that check radiation levels. That's not usually part of their gear."

Alexander sat back and let Lloyd's words sink in.

When they finally landed, they found Alexander's father had kept his promise. A sergeant was waiting to escort them off the tarmac to another a few feet away. A military Cessna usually reserved for transporting generals and higher-ranking officials on small jaunts was waiting for them. Alexander's dad was tied in through the old boy network of the military. They landed in Glasgow without complications.

As Rebekah and Alexander grabbed their gear, Lloyd bought a Land Rover from an airport worker. Bandit, Rocky, and Bear were glad to stretch their legs after the two long flights. Lloyd let them run in the grassy knolls that adjoined the Glasgow airport to the countryside.

Once they had settled into the vehicle, Rebekah said from the back seat, "I don't think we need to check his flat on campus. I'm sure it's been searched already. We can check his castle. It's about a two-hour drive."

Lloyd followed her directions as he drove through the lowlands. Occasionally they would see a shepherd leading his flock in for the night from pastures that dotted the woods that surrounded the road. Seeing the sheep, the dogs became excited and their barks resounded throughout the car. The sun was setting as they saw the silhouette of the 1,200-year-old castle sitting atop the hills overlooking the highland moors. All that could be seen was the very top turret and the gargoyles, which kept watch over the ancient stone fortress. As they drew closer, they could see the cold gray exterior. It was set in a middle of a clearing that retreated some 500 yards from the surrounding woods.

The mist was rising off the moors, which engulfed the castle. The stone exterior heated up during the day, causing the moors to cool down, resulting in a mist, disappearing the castle.

"Brigadoon," Lloyd muttered.

"What?" Rebekah asked, leaning up from the back seat.

"It reminds me of Brigadoon," Lloyd said.

"Actually I was thinking more of a movie called *Dracula*," Alexander replied, thinking about druids and *Dungeons and Dragons*. He figured this castle had dungeons; hopefully it didn't have dragons.

The muck of the moors sunk the Land Rover's tires, but could not stop the heavy vehicle. When they reached the driveway, Rebekah jumped out. She opened a faux stone panel next to the front door. She entered a code and the big oak doors swung open.

"Pretty high tech," Alexander said.

"Angus had the whole place wired. He wanted no problems. He has a generator in the cellar and extra storage batteries. We could hold up here for a hundred years. There's a stockpile of food and other supplies," Rebekah explained

"Cool. I like his style," Lloyd said as they entered the large foyer, which spanned three stories high.

"It's really quite charming once you get inside," Rebekah said. "Angus's family has kept it in great shape throughout the centuries. Because we're so far from the main road, there hasn't been much wear and tear from visitors. There's a diesel generator in the cellar and Angus always kept it filled to run electricity. It's actually quite comfortable."

A tapestry depicting a hunting scene hung down from a brass rod borne into the ceiling. A suit of armor stood at attention next to the base of the wide oak staircase. Rebekah walked through the hallway into the main great room where there was an eight-foot wide fireplace. Alexander threw logs on the grate and lit them.

"This fireplace keeps the room pretty warm," Rebekah said. "We can camp out in here and save the fuel to run the computers."

They followed her into the kitchen. She opened the pantry and grabbed some canned soup. Using a kerosene stove, she heated it up in a large saucepot. After they ate, Lloyd pulled on his coat. "I'm going outside," he said. As he opened the door, they heard the distant howl of a wolf.

"Don't go too far. The children of the night are calling you," Alexander said in a Boris Karloff voice.

"I hope we run into some wolves. The dogs need the exercise," Lloyd replied as he opened the back door while the dogs danced around him. The Australian shepherds were fierce fighters who would defend their owners to death and have fun doing it.

Walking back into the great room, Rebekah and Alexander sat down at the computer. The fire was blazing nicely and filled the room with a warm glow. She loaded a USB drive with programs and then deleted them from the computer's hard drive so no one else could get a copy. Then she opened up the chaotic correlator program. The test Angus had entered using all the world's religions came up. "The last thing Angus told me was that the one correlation he found was the phrase, 'in the beginning was the word,'" Rebekah said. "I've been trying to figure out what it means."

"The Bible refers to the word as Jesus. The Muslims refer to the word as Muhammed. Every religion had a prophet. The word in the form of a deity or a person spreading the gospel of that religion," Alexander said. "I'm not surprised that would be the correlation, because everything that begins and ends with communication—spoken or written—would be the tie between all mankind."

"But it specifically says the word is an entity, not a communication tool," Rebekah said.

"The Bible is a beautiful book of metaphors and can be interpreted many different ways. I mean, look at all the different religious sects," Alexander said.

"That's where faith comes in. You pray and have faith as you read," Rebekah said.

"Faith has nothing to do with it. It all ties back to communication," he said. "The words are speaking to us. We just need to understand what they're saying."

"Why would anyone want to kill him over a couple Bible verses?" Rebekah asked.

"Maybe it's not Bible verses. Maybe there's something you're missing. Maybe it's not about the program but about him," Alexander said.

***

Lloyd strolled through the woods, enjoying the mist that rose up and the hazy cloud covers. The air was fresh and green. Bear, Rocky, and Bandit darted off, chasing field mice, and then ran back to him. Lloyd felt all alone. He had wandered for a while, but could still make out the castle rising in the distance behind him. There wasn't a single soul in miles.

From his hilltop vantage, he could see the approaching headlights of what looked like three vehicles. Because of the terrain and distance, Lloyd figured he had at least thirty minutes before they reached the castle. They couldn't possibly be friendly visitors this far out from the village at this time of the night. The dogs barked and ran back toward the castle. That was when he saw the first wolf.

The wolf's eyes glowed red in the dim twilight. The first pair was joined by three more sets of eyes. He slowly reached behind his back to pull out his nine millimeter, which was hidden by his pea coat. Before he could grab it, a fifth set of eyes jumped and knocked him to the ground. The wolf tore at his arm and chest as he tried to fend it off. Bandit jumped on the wolf, knocking him off Lloyd. She lay the wolf on its back and tore at its throat so ferociously, so intensely that Lloyd took a step back, rising to his feet. Bear and Rocky took on the rest of the pack. He pulled out his nine millimeter, but was unable to shoot for fear of hitting one of his dogs. Instead he began hitting and pounding and pulling them off his Aussies. When he finally had a clear shot, he took out two wolves with two shots. The other three wolves took off with Bear and Rocky hot on their heels. He called after them, but they were too far gone. He watched as they vanished into the moonlight. The dogs had tasted blood and wanted to finish their job. Bandit stayed by his side, circling him and baring her teeth. She was torn between defending her pups and defending her master. He started to run off into the woods after them when he noticed that Bandit was limping and favoring her right hind leg. It had been torn open. He picked her up and carried her back to the castle.

Rebekah and Alexander had run out of the castle when they heard the shots. Alexander saw the flashlight, even though he couldn't make out the form. He heard Lloyd cry out. He ran to him and grabbed Bandit. Lloyd, too, had been torn up. His jacket was in shreds. He was bleeding from his neck to his arm. "Lloyd, what happened? We heard gunshots."

"Wolves. Bear and Rocky took off after them. Bandit's hurt pretty bad."

"What about you? You're covered in blood."

Lloyd gasped for air. "I'm okay. It's mostly wolf blood. Bandit's pretty bad. We have to patch her up and get out of here."

"The wolves aren't gonna get us in the castle."

"Not those kind of wolves. These walk on two legs. I saw headlights coming up the path along the river. They're about twenty minutes away right now. I'm sure they heard the gunshots."

Rebekah ran back into the castle to grab the drive and a bag full of food. She took one last look around the great room. There had been many great nights around this fireplace with her mentor and friend. She knew in her heart this would be the last time she would see the Castle McLean. On her way out, she grabbed a towel and blanket to wrap Bandit in.

Alexander drove as Rebekah and Lloyd worked on Bandit. They put on a tourniquet to stop the bleeding. She was motionless, although every now and then she would raise her head and lick Lloyd. She was more concerned about cleaning him. Eventually the dog passed out from exhaustion. Rebekah cleaned up Lloyd's wounds. As they left the clearing, the full moon allowed enough light to see along the trail so Alexander could make out ten feet ahead of him. Turning his head back slightly to the others, he said, "I'm killing the lights. We're going to have to drive within fifty feet of them to get back."

As he turned his head back, he slammed on his brakes as he saw two blurs of motion fly in front of the truck. And then they were standing on top of his hood, wiggling their butts and panting heavily. Alexander got out and let them in the cargo area. Their mouths were full of fur and blood. He had a feeling retribution had been made. Alexander jumped back in the car and took off. The two pups lay down by their mother and went to sleep.

Alexander pulled the Land Rover off the trail and down into the thicket. He turned off the engine. Ten minutes later, the three black Suburbans drove past them without stopping. When they were clear, Alexander pulled back onto the path, but he didn't turn the lights on until they were at least a mile away.

Outside Nairobi, Kenya

Even with the air conditioning blasting, the hot African sun beat down on the truck, keeping the interior around ninety degrees. Amat was thankful that Ariet was asleep and Oleg was dozing off. This was quite a different trip from the first time he had arrived in Nairobi.

Then he had been a newlywed on his way to the University of Nairobi with his new bride, Wannjiko. They were from the same village and attended the same school taught by Catholic missionaries. The missionaries had helped him get a scholarship to the university and his wife followed him there. After he completed his education, they had gone back to Sudan to help educate the children. They had started school programs in their own and neighboring villages. When the war intensified between northern and southern Sudan, he was drafted and given the position of commander. His education had helped him achieve high rank in the army. He was the only soldier in his squad who could actually read. He loved his country and was willing to die for it, but he wasn't willing to kill for it. He was a man of peace. Some other officers accused him of being weak, and they even whispered "coward."

After being away for a month on a training mission, he returned to his village to find it deserted and burnt to the ground. He searched the remaining huts and found no one until he got to the school, which was made out of bricks fashioned from the African mud. The doors and windows were boarded and locked. He kicked in a window and entered. Inside were the charred remains of the entire village. Children were huddled in a corner and burnt beyond recognition. He saw one family that appeared to be a mother covering the remains of four small children hiding behind the desk. On her left finger was a gold wedding band, on her right hand was a University of Nairobi class ring.

After two days of burying the village, Commander Amat led a squad of ten men across the Nile into northern Sudan to track the northerners that had razed the village. This was a direct violation of his orders. It was nighttime when they reached the northern Sudanese, who were sitting around a fire sharing stories and laughing.

Amat motioned for his squad to put their guns away. He drew out his maloda, a crudely made machete. Bullets would be too merciful. The first soldier Amat reached was drinking tea. Amat stuck the machete so far into his skull that he had to use both his feet to hold the head down as he pulled it back out. The massacre continued hours after the bodies were dead. That night, the great teacher had not crossed the Nile. It had to be someone or something else that could enact such horror.

Washington, DC

Mr. Stanley sat in his Pentagon office and picked up the ringing phone.

"Mr. Stanley, the professor won't be coming to Washington. He was killed while trying to escape."

"Did you get the program?"

"The mainframe was cleared. We were unable to retrieve any files including the program."

Mr. Stanley hung up the phone.

Despite visits to several other containment camps, Mr. Stanley had been unable to find the computer experts he needed to keep the country running. Things had gone from bad to worse. The term "martial law" could no longer hide the fact that the government had torn up the Bill of Rights. Houses were being invaded, civilians were being held without representation, and the hoarding and looting had gone out of control. A healthy black market was thriving.

Mr. Stanley turned to his picture of President Nixon. "What this country needs is a good war to get things back on track," he said. "It'll get their minds off their troubles. We have to get Betty in Iowa standing and saluting the flag again; when you have people sitting around instead of working, they think too much. That can be dangerous."

War was good for the country, Mr. Stanley believed. It lit the spark of patriotism, kept the economy going, and it was damn good fun. Yes, it was a little messy—that's why he preferred nukes. They left little behind. He had practically given away Tomahawk missiles to the Palestine Liberation Army. It was his idea to feed the fire in the Middle East, but the war wasn't big enough yet. The American people were still thinking too much. "Come in," he said when he heard the knock on the door.

Jim, one of his brighter Forced Volunteer Agents, walked in. "Sir, we have reports from Glasgow. She was there, but by the time the agents got there she was gone. She had deleted everything on the mainframe."

Mr. Stanley pounded his desk, knocking over a container full of neatly sharpened pencils. He stood staring at the pencils for a moment until he couldn't stand it any longer. Then he placed each one carefully into their place. He noticed some were not as sharp as others, so he took time to place them into his electric pencil sharpener. He measured one against the other until all their points were exactly the same. He emptied the shavings into the wastebasket he kept in the bottom drawer. It bothered him to have any kind of garbage that close to him, but he kept it for emergencies like this.

"How are they getting around? Every airport is being watched. Why do we keep missing them?" Mr. Stanley asked.

Jim shook his head. "I don't know, sir. Every non-military flight has been grounded."

"Bring in Kenny Maslow," Mr. Stanley said.

A short time later, Jim walked in with Kenny, who had been promoted due to his meticulous record-keeping skills. From that day in Soldier Field when he first saw Kenny's name, Mr. Stanley had earmarked him for greatness and brought him to the Pentagon.

"Sit down," Mr. Stanley said. "Jim, you can go." The guard walked out the door, closing it with a click.

Kenny sat in a leather chair, facing the cherry-wood desk. "Good morning," he said with a nervous lisp.

"Kenny, I've heard good things about you. The department is looking for ambitious young men like yourself."

"Thank you, Mr. Stanley," Kenny replied. "I feel it's the duty of all Americans to help out where they can."

"That's very admirable. I've noticed from your records you were a student at the University of Chicago before you entered the FVA."

"Yes, sir," Kenny replied. "I was majoring in ancient languages with a minor in computers."

"Ancient languages—that's interesting." Mr. Stanley said. "How'd you get involved in computer programming? It seems like two very different fields of study."

"Well, Mr. Stanley, they're really quite similar. Computers are just another language—perhaps the purest of all. My thesis was comparing the similarities between computer languages and ancient languages."

"Perhaps you can help me. I'm looking for a professor who taught at the University of Chicago. Her name is Rebekah Simmonds. She taught in the math department."

"I know who she is," Kenny replied, eager to help.

"Any ideas of how we could reach her? She's very important to the department."

Kenny thought for a moment. "I know she was working on a project with my professor. A project I should have been involved in."

"Go on..." Mr. Stanley encouraged him.

"When Professor Talcott returned from Africa, we were to work on his project together, categorizing the tribal languages of Sudan. I did all the grunt work for him before he left. I was his assistant. No, his partner," Kenny corrected himself. "Until she came along."

Mr. Stanley interrupted him. "Sometimes true geniuses aren't recognized. After all, she's a professor; you were merely a student. I've seen what you've achieved in our department. I can assure you your talents won't be wasted here."

Kenny sat for a moment, relishing the compliment, and then told Mr. Stanley about Professor Talcott and his relationship with Professor Simmonds. Even about Alexander's father.

Mr. Stanley stopped Kenny as he continued talking. "Thank you," he said, dismissing him. "When you leave, send Jim in."

Kenny walked out and Jim walked in. "Yes, Mr. Stanley?" Jim asked.

"Send for Mr. Doe," he said to Jim, tapping his fingers on the desktop.

30,000 Feet over the English Channel

"How bad are the bugs and snakes?" Rebekah asked Alexander. They were in the back section of the aircraft, normally reserved for officers. They had reached Heathrow hours ahead of schedule. They didn't want to take a chance flying, instead driving the back roads. They thought the military plane, which was set up by Alexander's dad, would be safe.

"Seeing as it's the rainy season, we may see a few," Alexander said. "You'll love the people in the villages. They're beautiful. Very warm and generous. I'm hoping you can meet Amat." Alexander glanced through the emailed pages of the scroll. Rebekah peered over his shoulder. She studied the writing for a few minutes.

"Who were these people?" Rebekah asked

"The key is the six scrolls. I'm hoping Amat is working on translating them. He deciphered the first one, which should make it easier to decipher the rest. I think the answer is in those scrolls," Alexander said. "A lot of what we found up to now hasn't made sense. We need to find a different way of looking at what we're seeing. The world's falling down around us and so far technology is losing."

"What are we losing to? Why is everything shutting down?"

"Maybe technology has a shelf life. Cultures come and go. Ideas come and go. People always survive. Now we have to find a way to survive," Rebekah said. "I've been working on a theory. All the computer systems around the world are shutting down. There's no virus, no damage."

"At least that anyone can see," Alexander interjected.

"It's almost like they're wearing out. As fast as programmers can reprogram, they stop again. What if we've reached the edge of the envelope of where computers can take us? What if we've finally overloaded the system and started a chain reaction? With the worldwide web and global communication and text messaging. What if that's all there is?"

"If it's not a virus, if it's not something manmade, what is it?"

"I don't know; no one knows. There are no foreign bodies in the program. No corruption. Every program is doing what it is supposed to do. It's like our languages are wearing out or maybe we've lost our ability to understand," Rebekah said.

"Think about it—think about the actual technology of communications," Lloyd said, coming and sitting down by them. "There's something ethereal about it. Back when we first transmitted radio waves through the air and then television, it seemed like magic, and now ones and zeros flying around the earth faster than the speed of light, crashing into atoms. It *is* magic."

"Well, if it's magic, how do you explain it? The writers of the scroll couldn't explain it—they wrote about how people weren't communicating with each other. They started wars because of misunderstandings," Alexander said. "Think of other mythical cultures like Atlantis, Xanadu, and Utopia. Man reached such an ultimate expansion of his science and culture it turned in on itself and he traded his soul for knowledge."

Rebekah rubbed her cross. "God created us in his own image because he wanted companionship. We haven't exactly been good companions, have we? Even Adam and Eve traded their souls for knowledge. We crucified his son, denigrated his church, polluted his creation, including our own bodies, with drugs, tattoos and cigarettes. We even kill in his name. Maybe just like our brothers in that cave, we've reached our limit."

Alexander sat and thought about her words. "The question is what do we do about it?"

"That's the problem. I can theorize. Every culture in history has its own lexicon. It's a way of communicating. It's a way of thinking. Culture's existence is shaped and developed by what that lexicon is. The lexicon is just a group of words or ideas that share a similar purpose. I think the computers have lost their lexicon. I think we lost our original lexicon a long time ago."

Outside Loki, Kenya

Amat pulled over to the side of the road. He yawned and stretched. The sun was playing hide and seek with the distant hills. They had been driving all day, and he couldn't tell if they were any closer to the border. The landscape had stayed the same: teak trees, elephant grass, kiosks of little food shops, and masses of people carrying their meager belongings along the roadside. Most of the food shops were closed. Some had been looted. "I thought we would rest here," Amat said, turning to look at Oleg and Ariet, who was just waking up.

He put the pistol in the back seat with Oleg. "Be careful, it's loaded," he said, reaching for the door handle. "I'll be right back."

"Where are you going?"

"To get us some food. Lock the doors until I come back." He stepped out of the car and closed the door. He waited to hear the click before he walked away. He had seen a fruit and vegetable kiosk about a half-mile back and walked towards it. The kiosk was made from corrugated metal with a thatched roof. As he walked up, an old man came out and said, "All I have left are two sweet potatoes."

"I'll take them."

"That'll be 10,000 shillings."

"For two sweet potatoes? All I have is 8,000." Amat emptied his wallet.

"Fine," the old man said, taking Amat's money and handing him the two steaming sweet potatoes. Carrying his treasure carefully, Amat walked back to the Range Rover. He knocked on the window. The doctor opened the door. Ariet was now sitting in the passenger seat. He handed one potato to the doctor and one to Ariet. "Where's yours, Amat?" she asked.

"I ate mine on the way back from the market." Amat sat back in the driver's seat and started the engine.

Ariet and Oleg silently devoured their meal as Amat continued down the road. When she finished the potato, skin and all, Ariet caught Amat starting to snooze at the wheel. "Pull over. I can drive," she said.

"It's going to get dark soon."

"I'd rather risk the roads than stay in this place." Pulling to the side of the road, they changed places. Amat stretched out in the passenger seat, his deep brown eyes centered on Ariet. The moonlight danced off her smooth ebony skin, revealing a privileged woman.

She hunched over the steering wheel, straining to watch for potholes and dangerous road creatures. His last thought as he drifted off to sleep was of brandishing a sword, defending his Nubian princess like his ancestors might have before him.

His head hit the windshield when she slammed on the brakes. His eyes flew open. The sudden glare of headlights not more than twenty feet in front of them temporarily blinded him.

Amat reached over and grabbed the steering wheel. He pulled it hard to the left as his foot covered hers and floored the gas pedal. "Bandits," he yelled as the sound of a machine gun fired behind them.

"What do I do? What do I do?" Ariet held her hands up from the steering wheel.

"Keep your foot on the gas. They can't possibly match our speed in their car," Amat replied. "And put your hands back on the steering wheel."

Ariet did as she was told. The Range Rover flew over potholes. At fifty miles per hour, it felt like a hundred. After five minutes, the headlights behind them faded into the distance. It was ten minutes before they realized that Oleg had not spoken or moved in a while.

With shaky hands, Ariet pulled the vehicle to the side of the road. "Papa, Papa," Ariet called as she climbed into the back seat. She clasped her hand over the hole in his back, trying to hold back the gush of blood. A ricocheting bullet had hit a main artery. Amat climbed behind her and started CPR. She tore pieces of her dress to act as a makeshift bandage. The material quickly turned from white to crimson as she tried to stop the tide. They both knew their attempts were futile, but neither could stop. Stopping meant he really was dead.

"Papa, Papa, no," Ariet cried as she leaned over her father, sobbing.

Amat pulled her off and brought her into his arms. "I'm sorry, Ariet." He stroked her hair as he gave a quick look behind them. "We must go."

"What about Papa?"

"We'll give him a proper burial when we get to Loki."
Amat climbed into the front seat. Ariet stayed in back, cradling
her father. Amat tried to start the car, but it only made a
grinding sound. The starter kicked on, but the engine refused to
click over. "I don't get it. It says empty, but I filled the gas." He
went out to look. As he stepped out of the car, his foot landed
in a pile of mud. When he walked to the back of the car, he saw
a puddle of liquid pooled under the gas tank. He smelled. It was
definitely gas. He looked closely. A bullet hole had punctured
the gas tank. *Thank God it didn't explode,* he thought. He looked
into the horizon. The sun would be rising shortly and he could
see the lights of Loki in the distance. It couldn't be more than
seven or eight kilometers. The rain turned to a gentle drizzle. It
was warm, but slightly cooler than the air. It gave some relief as
he raised his face to the sky. He got lost in the moment and said
a silent prayer to his ancestors. He did not have much faith in
prayer, especially to dead relatives he had never met, but it
seemed their luck had run out. Now he had to face Ariet and
tell her they had to leave her father behind.

"Ariet, we must go now," Amat said, looking in the back
seat.

"I can't leave Papa," Ariet said, staring at him, tears
glistening down her face. Her arms were still wrapped around
her father, her shirt covered in his blood.

"The car's out of gas. I can't leave you here to go get help.
We have to walk the rest of the way to Loki."

"I can't leave without my father."

"Don't you think your father would want you to be safe?"

"I'm not leaving without him."

"I can't leave you here."

"But I've lost everything. I've lost my home, my friends.
Now my father. I have nothing to go back to and I have
nothing to go forward to. I'll stay here."

Amat put a gentle hand on her shoulder. "We must go,
Ariet. We must go."

She closed her eyes and said a silent goodbye to her father. She knew she had to go, that it was what he would want. After she got out of the vehicle, they locked the doors and pushed the car into the tall elephant grass so it would be camouflaged. "If we can get a ride back, we will come back. I promise you," Amat said.

Ariet didn't acknowledge him. Amat gathered the scrolls, the satellite phone, and their water bottles. He took Ariet's hand and they began the slow trek to Loki.

Ariet took one glance back at the Range Rover and said a silent prayer for her father. "How far is it?" she asked, shielding her eyes from the rising sun. The rain was tapering off and giving way to the sun.

"I'd say it's about seven kilometers," Amat said, leading the way through the roadside mud. This highway was usually crowded with cars, but now there were none to be seen.

Cairo, Egypt

They could feel the heat off the tarmac before the plane touched the ground. Distorted images danced off the steaming asphalt. Steam bubbled off the surface, bouncing back to be reflected off the plane's steel. The plane touched down with a bouncing jerk and came to a screeching stop on a runway that was too short. Looking outside, Rebekah noticed that the air base was a contradiction of worlds. It didn't quite fit into this desert landscape. There were F16 fighter planes parked next to camels. It was a makeshift base dropped into an ancient world.

As US planes landed, the American flag was covered by the blue flag of NATO. Soldiers marched by the airfield. They were all garbed in gray with the blue patch, but were of every nationality. Every country had joined the New World Order except Israel. The Israelites stood undaunted, surrounded by enemies for centuries. Now, as they prepared to fight their final battle with their enemies close at hand, they still refused to fly the NATO flag.

Rebekah looked around as she stepped out of the aircraft cabin. She wanted to withdraw back into the cool cabin to escape the oppressive heat, but there was no turning back. One of the soldiers handed her a hooded veil as she followed Alexander to the waiting cars. "Ma'am, you'll have to wear this if you leave the base."

"Thank you," she said, pulling the silky material through her fingers.

"I'm Corporal Hennessy. I've been assigned to take care of you. First I need to bring you to the colonel," the young man said to Rebekah and Alexander. Lloyd was busy unloading the dogs. "Please follow me." He led them to a Humvee.

They all watched as Lloyd got the heavily panting dogs together. It was only six in the morning but already felt like ninety degrees. "You get used to the heat, ma'am," the corporal said. Suddenly, Bear and Rocky took off, chasing a flock of sheep in the distant sand.

Lloyd called after them. "Looks like they'll fit in right here," he said to Alexander. Bandit stayed by Lloyd's side. The two young puppies were a sight to be seen. They were nipping at the sheep's paws and leading them right into a circle. They worked as a team and were not satisfied until all the sheep were rounded up. Then the puppies ran back to Lloyd, tongues hanging out of their mouths, butts wiggling. "Good job," he said, patting them.

Alexander and Rebekah climbed into the Humvee. Lloyd jumped on the back with the three dogs crowding around him. They drove around the dusty roads. Rock music was blaring as soldiers walked around. An impromptu baseball game was going on in a clearing. "If you need anything, let me know. You guys must be connected, because you've got carte blanche around the base. But there are two things," the corporal said. "Don't leave the compound after dark, and check your shoes before you put them on. We've got a bad scorpion problem."

"Is there a good scorpion problem?" Lloyd asked, leaning forward.

"We most likely won't be staying long. Neither should be a problem," Alexander said.

They arrived in front of a makeshift building. Its sides were corrugated aluminum, its roof some type of grass, and the foundation concrete. "Wait here. I'll be right back." The corporal jumped out and ran inside. A few minutes later, the corporal stuck his head out and waved them inside. They walked into the commander's office. He was a man in his fifties with dark hair and a muscular build.

"Colonel, the civilians are here," the corporal said, snapping a salute.

The colonel returned the salute and stood up. "Welcome to my base. I'm Colonel Irwin. We've got quarters set up for you. Corporal Hennessy will be responsible for you while you're on the base. After that you're on your own."

Alexander cut in. "Actually, we're not planning on being here that long, sir. We're hoping to secure transportation to take us to southern Sudan."

"Son, that's impossible. The fighting is intense—no one is getting in or out. Even without the fighting, southern Sudan is impassible right now because of the rain."

"Can you just tell us the best place to go to find transportation?"

"Look, son, I'd like to help you. I received word from Washington to do my best to accommodate you, but I've got a war going on. We are the supply line to the front. I need every man and machine here for the war in Israel. And to boot, there are tribal wars breaking out in every African country and in Iraq. I've got to play peacekeeper, police officer, and soldier. Frankly, son, I can't help you out."

"What about civilian transportation?" Lloyd asked.

"All civilian transportation has been stopped because of the war. You're our guests. You've been grounded here until further notice," the colonel said.

"This bites," Lloyd said, standing up. "We didn't fly halfway around the world to be babysat by GI Joe. I don't think so." He stormed out.

"Excuse him, Colonel. Thanks for your time." Alexander stood up followed by Rebekah. As they walked out, the colonel picked up the phone and called Washington. On the other end of the line, a perfectly manicured hand lifted the receiver. "They're here," the colonel said into the phone. "Do you want me to detain them?"

"No," the other voice said, clicking down the receiver. All the colonel heard was a dial tone.

Alexander and Rebekah walked over to Lloyd, who was standing by the Humvee, stroking the dogs.

"Look, I don't know about you guys, but I'm not sticking around here. Let's head to town and find us a ride," Lloyd said.

"I'm in," Alexander replied.

"Me, too," Rebekah said. They jumped back into the Humvee.

"Sorry about that, folks," the corporal said, climbing back into the driver's seat.

"That's okay. We would like to head into town to take a look around," Alexander said. "It seems like we will be stuck here a while, so I would like to make the most of it."

"We can't guarantee your safety outside the compound," the corporal replied, starting the engine. "I'll have to ask the colonel first."

"I'll be responsible for our safety," Alexander replied. "You said we have carte blanche."

"All right," the corporal said with a shrug. He called and held out his hand to two privates playing volleyball. They ran over.

"Yeah, Corporal," a lanky blonde boy said.

"Get your gear. We're going into town," the corporal commanded.

"You got it." The privates ran off and came back a few minutes later carrying machine guns and wearing full camouflage. Half an hour later, they arrived in the nearby village called Kishna. The marketplace was crowded with people and livestock. Most of the merchants had no goods for sale but were instead standing and arguing with each other. Egyptian police bearing machine guns were breaking up the arguments and urging everyone to go home. As the corporal stopped the Humvee, Rebekah put her veil on. Alexander smiled and squeezed her hand. "It gives you that *1001 Nights* look. I think I like it," he whispered so the others wouldn't hear.

"Don't be a wiseass. You try breathing through this."

The two puppies jumped out of the Humvee and started chasing a herd of sheep. Bandit watched her puppies. She seldom left Lloyd's side, but her puppies were always looking for something to do. Lloyd thought about calling them but decided to let them run. With skill and precision, Bear and Rocky bumped and herded the sheep through the busy marketplace and into a holding pen. When the merchant saw the dogs' nipping at his sheep's heels, he grabbed a stick. Before he could lower the stick, a hand grabbed him. The merchant's face flushed with anger until a flash of recognition crossed over him. Standing over him was Sheik Abdul Rahad, the third richest oil sheik in Egypt. His wealth was only surpassed by his father and older brother, who were number one and two.

The merchant immediately fell to his knees begging for forgiveness. Sheik Rahad waved him off and petted both puppies as they jumped and circled around him, wagging their tailless butts with unlimited enthusiasm. Lloyd had run from the Humvee when he saw the man raise his stick. Now he was standing before the sheik, wondering why everyone in eyeshot was kneeling in the sand. "Bear, Rocky," Lloyd called. The dogs hesitated as the sheik looked at Lloyd; his dark black eyes pierced his face and his cultured appearance was a contrast to the sand, dust, and dirt that covered the marketplace. He was wearing a perfectly tailored, dark blue Armani suit. "Are these magnificent animals yours?" he asked with an English accent that surprised Lloyd.

Lloyd smiled and said, "If you mean do they belong to me, the answer is no. They travel with me. As you can see, they have minds of their own."

The sheik returned the smile and nodded his head. "I know what you are saying. It's like you don't ride a good Arabian horse. He allows himself to be ridden. It's a partnership."

"I'm John Lloyd," Lloyd held out his hand.

The sheik stared at his hand for a second, before shaking it. "Join me for some tea. Tell me about these beautiful animals," the sheik said.

"Make it a beer and I will."

"You've got a deal," came the sheik's reply.

The two men walked off to a nearby café, leaving the three dogs in the Humvee. Rebekah and Alexander wandered around the marketplace followed by the soldiers. Alexander's frustration grew as they continuously were told "no" when he asked about transportation options. No one was willing to help. At any price. Hours passed. Rebekah and Alexander baked in the sun, eventually going to sit under a tree with the dogs, waiting for Lloyd. As the sun started to fade from the sky, the corporal walked up to them. "Look, we need to head back to base. You don't want to be caught out here after dark."

"What about Lloyd?" Rebekah spat through the thick veil.

"We'll take a quick walk. But if he's not back in fifteen minutes, we really need to go," the corporal said, looking at his watch. All the soldiers had been issued analog watches since the digital ones were not working.

"We can't just leave him here," Rebekah said.

"You don't understand," the corporal said, giving her a sharp look. "These are my orders, and I need to follow them. That Humvee is leaving with or without you in fifteen minutes."

Lloyd came running over, his Cubs cap replaced by an Egyptian hat. "Got great news," he said.

"Where'd you get that goofy-looking hat?" Alexander asked.

"No matter. I've got great news."

"Where have you been all day? We've been looking all over for you."

"Look, I traded." Lloyd pointed to the sheik, who was standing alongside a Mercedes Benz limo wearing the Cubs cap.

"I'm glad you made friends, but we've got to get out of here. We've been trying to find transportation, but there's none to be found," Alexander said.

"Don't worry about that. I've got it solved," Lloyd said, waving his hand. It was obvious he had been drinking. "My man the sheik is going to take us back to his place, and then we will explain everything."

The corporal walked over. "That's not possible," he said. "I have orders to escort you. I've taken responsibility for you."

"We'll take responsibility for us," Alexander said.

As they spoke, twenty of the sheik's armed guards encircled the Americans. "It's your funeral," the corporal said as he did a mental tally of the situation. The odds weren't in his favor. He walked over to the Humvee, followed by the two privates.

Alexander and Rebekah followed Lloyd to where the sheik was waiting. "Abdul, these are my friends, Becky and Al," Lloyd introduced them.

Alexander reached out to shake the sheik's hand. The sheik looked for a moment and shook his hand. He noticeably ignored Rebekah's hand. "Hmmm," Rebekah muttered under her breath and rewrapped the veil around her face.

"Welcome, my friends. Let me invite you to my home." Abdul snapped his fingers. The driver ran up and opened the door. Bear and Rocky were already in the limo, their panting faces hanging out the window. Alexander followed Rebekah and Lloyd and Bandit onto the leather seat.

"Tonight you will be my guests in my palace. We'll have a feast in your honor," the sheik said.

"Thank you," Alexander said, relishing the air-conditioned comfort.

"He's going to hook us up with transportation," Lloyd said.

After about twenty minutes driving through the dry sand, they pulled up in front of a beautiful palace. A Jaguar, Rolls Royce, and Land Rover were all parked in the circular drive in front of the doors. A Cessna and a private jet were parked next to the cars.

"Nice choice," Lloyd said, walking out of the car and looking at the Cessna.

"Do you fly?" The sheik walked up behind him.

"I've got 5,000 hours. I'm more of a weekend warrior."

"That's my son's plane. I fly the jets."

Abdul escorted Rebekah to the entrance of the women's area, which was separate from the main entrance. "You'll find fresh clothes there."

"Fine, whatever," Rebekah said as she was pulled inside by a chattering woman.

Lloyd and Alexander laughed. The three dogs jumped out of the limousine to chase a group of llamas. Lloyd whistled to call them back. "Let them go. They'll be safe on my land," Abdul said.

The sheik took them on a tour, displaying his Arabian horses and his award-winning sheep. "I only collect the best. The finest horses, the finest sheep, and the finest women."

"In that order?"

"A good animal is worth ten good women," the sheik replied with a wry smile.

They were called into dinner by tinkling music. Alexander and Lloyd tripped over the flowing robes they had borrowed for dinner. They ran into a freshly washed and veiled Rebekah outside the dining hall. "Our problems are over. We've got transportation," Lloyd said to Alexander.

"What do you mean?"

"Becky, quick; fold your arms and blink."

"Real funny, Lloyd." The three walked into dinner. It was normally not the custom of the house to allow a woman to eat with the men, but Lloyd had convinced the sheik that Rebekah wouldn't cause any trouble. However, she had to sit at the end of the table away from the others. The great dining hall was an eclectic mixture of British antiques and native artifacts. The sheik had told Lloyd he was schooled in England. He had shown them his cricket trophies. The three were pleasantly surprised not to eat monkey brains or some other exotic concoction. Instead they were treated to a seven-course gourmet meal ending with chocolate fondue. After the meal, the sheik bade goodbye to his guests and left the great hall.

Rebekah walked to where Alexander and Lloyd were sitting. "What now?"

"The custom is you do the dishes," Lloyd said.

"No, really, what do we do now?" Rebekah put her hands on her hips.

"The sheik has a war tribunal he's meeting with. He's trying to organize the tribes in case there's fighting."

"What about transportation?" Alexander asked.

"He said he would talk to us in the morning about it." Lloyd led the way out of the hall. The three parted ways and went to their rooms. Rebekah stopped to glance at herself in a mirror. She fought back the urge to cross her arms and blink. She had forgotten how good silk felt rubbing against her body. She had forgotten a lot of things about being a woman. She hoped she'd have time to remember before the whole world came crashing down.

***

Mr. Doe watched as each light shut off. He'd been watching them all day. He could have taken the girl and killed the American men at any time while they were in the marketplace. That would have been too easy. After all, he took pride in his work. Since the Berlin Wall had fallen, there hadn't been much need for him.

Oh, sure, there were still some presidential skeletons that needed covering—a few late night rendezvous that might have slipped—but it wasn't Cuba in the 60s or even Dallas. Now the New World Order did things out in the open, so there wasn't much need for a fixer. Now he had one last job—one last mess to clean up. He knew how much Mr. Stanley hated messes. Mr. Stanley didn't like things out in the open. And he didn't trust many people.

Mr. Doe lived to walk silent—the Viet Cong could walk through a jungle without being heard. He had learned to live in the shadows. He was a ghost!

Since this was his last big assignment, he decided to make it interesting. The sheik's palace was the ultimate challenge—its high walls, security cameras, and armed guards made it almost impregnable. He would slip in, take out the two American men, grab the girl and, for the hell of it, kill the sheik. And he'd make it look like the Israelis did it. Mr. Stanley would appreciate that; he wanted to pour some gasoline on the Middle East wars; that could possibly increase his bonus.

Plus there'd be the long trip back to Washington and the girl was very beautiful.

After quickly disposing of the three guards, he went first to the royal bedroom. The two Americans would be easy to take care of, but the sheik was a different story. He was a well-trained soldier himself. There were two armed guards wearing robes standing guard outside the bedroom. These royal palace guards were standing at attention. They would put up more of a fight than the perimeter guards. He was running short of time, so nothing fancy. He pulled out his ten-millimeter silencer and put a bullet in each head.

Seconds later he was inside the sheik's bedroom. The sheik was sound asleep underneath the canopy of his four-poster bed. The room was decorated with centuries of swords hanging on the ceiling and soft tapestries on the walls. Unfortunately, there was no time to challenge him; Mr. Doe hated killing the strong in their sleep. That tactic was normally reserved for the weak. They were worthless anyway. He was about to kill a great warrior. If he hadn't hesitated for that one instant, he might have been successful. Instead, by the time he heard the low growl behind him and turned around, it was too late. Rocky and Bear jumped and pounced on him, tearing at his throat. Hearing the noises, the sheik woke up and sounded the alarm. The pups tore at Mr. Doe. The sheik brandished a saber and called the dogs off. They held the intruder at bay until the sheik's men came and took Mr. Doe away.

"Is everything all right?" Alexander asked, rushing into the room. His room was two doors down from the sheik's. He was disheveled, wearing a pair of borrowed pajama bottoms. "I heard noises."

"Yes, my friend. My men have it under control, thanks to your friend's dogs. We had an intruder." The sheik walked over to Alexander. "We think he was after your friend."

"Lloyd?" Alexander asked, rubbing his tousled head.

"No, the woman. We found this on him." The sheik handled Alexander a picture. It was Rebekah standing outside the University of Chicago.

"Becky. Why would anyone want Becky?"

"I don't know, my friend."

"Can I call Washington?" Alexander asked.

"Be my guest. Use the satellite phone in my office. You will have privacy there."

Alexander walked down the hall, feeling the cool marble against his feet. He entered the sheik's Westernized office and sat behind the large mahogany desk. "Dad, it's me," Alexander said as his father picked up the phone.

"Alexander, where are you? Is everything all right? Colonel Irwin told me you didn't return to the base. What happened?" Colonel Talcott fired off questions.

"We're at Sheik Rahad's palace. Someone tried to kill him. The assassin was after Rebekah," Alexander said.

"Are you okay? Is she okay?

"Yes, we're safe," Alexander replied.

"The FVA is hunting down computer programmers or anyone that can help bring systems back online. I'm afraid all your lives are in danger," Colonel Talcott said.

"Those must have been the men that were after us in Scotland," Alexander said.

"That's what I've been trying to tell you, son. Rebekah's high on the list of FVAs. Something about some program she developed. You won't be safe anywhere now. I know who they sent after you. If they're willing to send him, they are willing to stop at nothing. Stay away from the military bases and get away from the city."

"I know. We're going to keep a low profile."

"Good."

Alexander paused, feeling his throat close. "Dad, I love you. We'll be okay. Watch your back. Don't let anyone know you talked to us."

"I love you too, son." The colonel hung up the phone with his left hand. In his right hand was a .45 caliber automatic that he kept ready at all times. He glanced through the blinds and saw the black suburban that had been parked there throughout the night.

***

The next morning, Rebekah saw Alexander walk outside to the sheik's desert garden. She went to join him. Lloyd was standing with Alexander. Bandit was standing beside them. "Let's go. I got us a ride," Lloyd said.

"What's your hurry?" Rebekah asked, noticing some brightness in his eyes.

"Let's go before I change my mind." Lloyd rushed to the Cessna.

"Change your mind about what?" Rebekah asked, following his frantic pace. "Where are Bear and Rocky?"

Lloyd paused and turned around to look at her. "They won't be coming along on this trip."

Loki, Kenya

Ariet looked around as they entered the city limits of Loki. The city had been built around the UN relief operations for Sudan. What had started as a small base now comprised a small city. There was a Paris fashion center, a native music store, and a barbecue restaurant. At one time they were probably thriving; now there were no goods or people to be seen. The windows of the stores were broken, signs were hanging down, and it looked as if the merchandise had been picked over by vultures.

She followed Amat past the wire barricade that led onto the airfield. There were no guards at the checkpoint. "What now?" Ariet asked as they stood on the muddy empty airstrip. The airbase was still—no planes could be seen.

"I don't know." Amat sat cross-legged on the hot tarmac. He had hoped to find Stan, his friend, to ask him to fly them into Sudan. Stan and his plane were missing. "Let me think a minute."

"I need some water," Ariet said, running a hand through her hair.

"There's a cantina two buildings over." Amat pointed.

"You think. I'll go find us a drink." Ariet walked toward where Amat had pointed. She walked to the steel hut and stopped in the doorway.

The silence of Amat's thoughts was interrupted by a piercing scream. He jumped up and ran to the cantina and Ariet. He pulled her into his arms. Looking around, he saw the sight that had unnerved her. Red splattered the walls. The bartender was bent over the bar, flies swarming around the caked blood on his back. Two headless men were sitting upright at a table near the bar like they were in mid-conversation. Their heads lay on the floor next to them. Slouched down in the corner, a barmaid was sliced open from her crotch to her throat. Her torso jerked like she was coming to life. A rat stuck its head out from her intestines. Ariet screamed again. As the stench invaded her nostrils, she threw up.

"Who could have done this?" Ariet asked, peering over Amat's shoulder as she clung to him.

He heard a faint sound from the office across the hall. Holding Ariet's hand, he walked over to the office to see Stan, lying on the floor clutching what was left of his stomach.

"Stan, what happened?" Amat bent down. He tore off his t-shirt and tried to bandage the open wound.

"That won't help, my friend," Stan said. "I'm already dead. Take my ring and send it to my wife." Stan held out his hand, giving him his signet ring, a remnant of his days with the Swedish Air Force.

"What happened? Who did this?" Amat bent down by Stan.

"People have gone mad. They're out of control," Stan gasped out. "Take the emergency kit. It's locked in the closet."

"Where's the key?" Amat pocketed Stan's ring.

"It's..." Stan pointed. His last breaths were causing him to lose the ability to talk. He gave one last gasp and then was gone. Amat laid his head down slowly and covered his face with the rest of the t-shirt. "How can this happen?" he asked. "My God, what is going on?"

He found the key to the closet taped to the side of the desk where Stan had pointed. He pulled down the emergency kit and went back to Ariet, who was standing stock-still, shaking. "We must leave," Amat said.

She shook her head, her arms wrapped around herself. "So much blood."

"Don't look. Hold my arm and walk." Amat shouldered the heavy kit and took Ariet's arm. She clung to him tightly.

As they left the office, Amat thought of a slaughterhouse he had once visited. Here was the same—pieces of what used to be a living creature scattered on the floor, dried blood on the walls, and the overpowering stench of something rotten. The grotesque shapes and pieces didn't look quite human. Amat looked away and maneuvered Ariet out the door. Ariet gasped for air when they got outside.

She dropped to the ground, her head bouncing lightly off the dirt, bile rising up through her throat. Amat kneeled down and picked her up. He placed the duffel bag over his shoulder. "At least I know the way walking around the jungle. At least in the jungle I know what animals I'm facing." He walked, carrying her towards the border.

Entering Sudan, Africa Airspace

Lloyd flew the plane, humming "Danger Zone" from *Top Gun*. It was one of his favorite movies. Bandit was pacing back and forth in the cockpit, her soft whimpers carried throughout the plane. "Settle down, girl," Lloyd said. "I miss them, too," he leaned over and whispered in her ears.

"What's our flight plan?" Alexander asked.

"Well, we don't really have any flight plan. We're going to fly as low and as far as we can, away from any major towns. We'll figure out how to land once we get there."

"Good flight plan. How do we avoid northern Sudan?"

"That's why we're flying low. So their radar doesn't pick us up. I just hope you can find the village once we land, Big Al."

"I hope so, too." Alexander sat down next to Rebekah.

"I don't understand why the government is willing to kill us over this program," she said.

"What is so different about it? You told me that it was developed to correlate unrelated data. What does the government want with a math program? All your papers have been about correlating religion, right, Becky?" Alexander asked.

Rebekah nodded. "I don't think the government is interested in God. There must be something that we're not seeing."

"My dad told me the military programs are crashing after nine hours. For some reason, each time the engineers write a new program, it degenerates at an increasing rate."

"That's it. That's the missing key," Rebekah said.

"What'd I miss?" Alexander asked.

"The heart of the chaotic correlator program is that it is self-teaching. In order to correlate unfamiliar data, it learns and reprograms itself instantaneously. The more it's used, the faster it works. It has the capacity for infinite knowledge and can never be obsolete," Rebekah explained.

"And you wrote this in your spare time as a grad student." He chuckled.

"Angus gets most of the credit. He and Albert were kicking around the idea of artificial intelligence before you and I were born. It's not a new concept. It's just the introduction of chaotic math opened up our minds so that we could conceive of this theory. You see, Alexander, communication begins with the way you perceive yourself and your surroundings. If you open your mind, the possibilities are endless."

Alexander looked at Rebekah with a new awe. She dangled names like Albert Einstein and Angus McLean like they were her old college roommates. She was in a fraternity that he would never be able to enter. He wasn't put off. He admired her. No, he was actually in love with her. "What if we just give them the program? We can send it to my dad."

Rebekah looked at him—eyes wide in shock. "Those bastards killed Angus. They tried to kill us. You want to just hand it over to them?"

"Not everyone in the government is corrupt. There are still some good men like my dad. What if we give him the program? We could stop this."

"It's too late for that. The times, they are a-changing, Alexander. What's happening now has nothing to do with computers." Rebekah fingered the cross around her neck, leaned back, and closed her eyes.

Alexander knew there was no arguing. He ran a hand over his cheek. He closed his eyes. He longed to hear the seventh inning stretch at Wrigley and enjoy a hot dog and beer. He could hear the crack of a bat while he yelled from the bleachers. He could smell the fresh-cut grass and hear the cry of the friendly confines, cheered by the bright blue sky, which was suddenly awash with a bright light.

"What was that?" Rebekah leaned forward to look out the cockpit window.

Lloyd fought to regain control of the aircraft. The plane was losing altitude. Their descent was rapid. "It was some sort of explosion," he yelled above the noise.

"What kind of explosion?" They heard a thunder-like ripple resound behind them.

"What the?" Alexander's words were interrupted by a roar that shook the plane as they held their ears. Bandit howled. Lloyd's nose bled. He hadn't had a nosebleed since he was a little boy.

"Are we being shot at?" Rebekah asked, looking out the window.

Lloyd shook his head. "The explosion was miles away."

"How do you know?" Alexander asked.

Lloyd pointed out the window. Alexander and Rebekah watched in horror as they saw the rising mushroom cloud. Lloyd tried to remember from every science fiction movie he had seen what the range of devastation was—ten miles, one hundred miles, one thousand miles. It didn't matter much, he guessed. Before he could fixate on or realize the magnitude, the plane started going down again.

"This is it. We're going in. I can't control it," Lloyd screamed, pushing buttons in a futile attempt to recover. He held the plane as best as he could. It skipped along the water like a perfectly round flat stone from a boy's hand. On the fourth skip, they bounced into the river and the plane filled up with water. The tail and left wing were gone and the fuselage split in two, which probably saved their lives. Alexander and Rebekah climbed out before most of the plane went down. They clung to pieces of seat cushions as Bandit dogpaddled next to them.

"Are you hurt?" Alexander called to Rebekah. He could see the shore a small distance ahead. She was struggling. The seat belt was wrapped around her waist. He swam through the murky water to free her. He pulled her out of the belt with one tug and placed her on a piece of the wing, which was floating among the debris. He looked for Lloyd and saw him floating facedown, still strapped to the pilot's seat. "Lloyd," Alexander called. Bandit was nipping at Lloyd's heels. There was no movement or noise from his old friend. He turned Lloyd over—his face was caved in. He swam back to Rebekah and held her tight. "Are you all right?" He ran his hands through her wet hair.

"I'm...okay," she gulped out. "Where's Lloyd?"

Alexander pointed, not wanting to explain more than he had to. "We're okay."

"Are we going to make it? What about radiation?" Rebekah clung to him as they sat on the wing drifting along to shore.

"I think we're far enough away that it shouldn't affect us." Alexander put his arm around her.

Rebekah cried and shook. She couldn't stop.

Washington, DC

Mr. Stanley sat across from the president in the Oval Office. He was tired of the secrecy. He was tired of the politics and most of all he was tired of the mess. Mr. Stanley listened to the president drone on about peace plans and rebuilding. It wasn't going to happen on his watch. Things had gone too far. Jerusalem was on fire; the clean-up had begun. Pretty soon, if Mr. Stanley had his way, the whole world would be clean again.

The president took a sip of his coffee and placed it back on his desk instead of on the saucer. Several drips splattered onto the cherry wood desk. The president continued, "I've been told by our experts that the NOMAD system has about nine hours left before shutting down completely. This time there will be no rebooting it. I've spoken to the Chinese…"

As the president talked, Mr. Stanley fixated on the drips on the desk. They were starting to dry and would leave a stain. He fought hard not to get up to wipe them. That would not be appropriate.

"...the United Arab Nations and the Europeans all agree," the president continued, "that the attack on Israel by the PLO was unforgivable. I think we can control the damage. I have agreed to disable our offensive nuclear attack devices. According to the secretary of defense, all the countries with nuclear capacity will do the same, and since all our systems are down to nine hours anyway, I think we can avoid any further destruction."

Mr. Stanley watched the last drip dry and harden on the desk. This was unforgivable. The damage had already been done. Israel was destroyed and so was the desktop. There was no going back. There was no damage control. Sure, the desk could be cleaned. There were polishes and wood care products that would hide that stain, but it would never be pristine again. Oh no, it was soiled now. It was unclean.

"Mr. Stanley, I will no longer be needing your services," the president continued. "The Forced Volunteer Agency is shut down."

Mr. Stanley thought about how his father had beaten him when he wet his bed. He had been in first grade. He eventually learned to control his messes. They were dirty little things that needed to be kept inside. But the beatings still came every night. "Dirty little boy," his dad would say as he reached for his belt.

The president reached into his pocket and pulled out a cigarette. Watching him, Mr. Stanley rubbed the cigarette burn scars on his arms. When his father was really drunk, the belt wasn't enough.

When the president stood up to show him out, Mr. Stanley picked up the letter opener on the desk that had been given to the president from the Russian ambassador. It was stainless steel, very shiny and clean. It gleamed and had an amber tip. He stuck it into the president's eye.

Sudan

The rain pooled around their ankles as they sloshed through the mud. Ariet screamed as she tried to step out of a particularly deep patch. Amat pulled her out. She had never been in the jungle before and every sight and noise startled her. Each crackle of the brush made her jump and grab onto Amat. She was glad he was with her. His calm assuredness comforted her.

Amat looked up. It was getting darker. They had better pitch their tent now. He looked for a clearing, but all he could see was tall elephant grass. Using his machete, he hacked at the grass. Finally he cleared enough to pitch their tent. They dined in silence on dried beef jerky and a ration of water. Outside the tent, the rain turned to a gentle drizzle.

"What's going to become of us? What's happening to our world?"

"I'm not quite sure." Amat stretched his legs to the end of the tent. "I don't know what is going on myself. When I talked to my friend in America, he said things were bad there also. It's all over the world. We've become so dependent on machines. We don't know how to live without them."

"What will we do here?"

"I was raised in the jungle. I know my way around. At least we'll be safe here."

"Will life ever be the same?"

"I don't know. If we can make it through the pass before the heavy mudslides, we'll be safe in the valley. In the rainy season, the valley is surrounded by water. There's only one way in. I hope it's not too late."

"And if it is?" Ariet's question hung in the air.

Along the Nile, Sudan

Rebekah and Alexander lay exhausted on the muddy banks of the shore. Their clothes clung to them and were caked with mud. Their breath came out in short, shallow tones. Bandit stood next to them, staring out at the plane's wreckage as it slowly sunk into the Nile, carrying its passenger on his last ride. The dog broke into a mournful howl. Rebekah and Alexander watched in silence.

"Where do you think we are?" Rebekah asked.

"Just before the explosion, Lloyd said we were entering southern Sudan airspace. Then the bomb went off." Both looked up and saw the ash-filled sky.

"I never thought it would come to this." Rebekah leaned against Alexander. He braced her with his shoulder. Bandit leaned against Rebekah's side, whining softly. "She misses Lloyd," Rebekah said, running her hands along the dog's soft, still damp fur.

"And the pups." Alexander reflected for a moment. He missed Lloyd and his sense of humor.

"Where do we go from here?"

"I need to get my bearings. We need to see if we can find our survival kit so we have some supplies." Alexander stood up and stretched. He scanned the muddy water, looking at all the alien metal floating around. Finally he saw a piece of the rear cabin drifting against the shore. "Maybe I can find some of our gear over there." He walked over to it. Rebekah followed him and stood on the shore as he waded toward the metal. When he reached the plane, Alexander climbed onboard, slipping along the sleek metal, trying to find a foothold. He went inside and found what he was looking for—the carefully packed survival kit that Lloyd had gathered for them. He threw things out to the shore. Rebekah hauled the stuff in and piled them up around her. Bandit circled around her, barking madly. Rebekah saw something move out of the corner of her eye.

"Alexander, be careful," she called. She couldn't make the shape out in the dim light. Night was starting to close in.

"What is it?" Alexander stood on the remaining metal that wasn't submerged.

"Over there. I saw something move." Rebekah pointed.

"I don't see anything," Alexander said, reaching with his hand to hold the metal while he stepped back into the water. He saw a long tail spiraling towards him. He fell in the murky water. The tail moved closer to him. Then it was gone. From his jungle survival training, he knew the most dangerous crocs were the ones you couldn't see. They submerged when they were about to attack. From that split second, it had looked to be about seven to eight feet long. He frantically looked around the waist-high water. He half ran, half swam the thirty feet back to shore. But when he was about ten feet away, the crocodile surfaced between him and the shore. Rebekah screamed. His heart was beating so fast he couldn't swallow. Bandit jumped into the water. With great leaps, the old Aussie had the crocodile's tail in her mouth. The crocodile thrashed around ferociously, trying to shake off the 65-pound Aussie. A lesser dog would have let go, but Bandit didn't know how to give up. It was bred in her through generation after generation. Alexander grabbed a piece of jagged fuselage that was floating nearby. He hit the croc straight between its eyes. It rolled over and took off. Bandit and Alexander swam to shore.

Alexander fell to his knees as Rebekah ran over to him. "Are you okay?" She fell onto the sand next to him. "I can't believe it. It's a real crocodile."

"You're going to find a lot of real stuff out here," Alexander gasped out, breathing heavily.

As she patted him down, his heart started to pound again—this time for a different reason. Their eyes met. They leaned in closer but were interrupted when they heard the pained whimpering of Bandit. Alexander went over to the brave dog, who was having a hard time breathing. He ran his hands over her to find out where she was injured. When he had his hand on her belly, she let out a loud whimper. "What is it?" Rebekah asked.

"The croc must have injured her rib. I can't tell if it is broken or not."

"Can she walk?"

"Hopefully, by morning. We'll set up camp here for the night. We can't travel after dark," Alexander said. A gentle rain fell as they moved away from the shore. Alexander recognized a mud hut near them. It was engraved with lizards and other native creatures. He thought they must be on the Ethiopian and Sudanese border. On the Sudan side. That meant a fifty-mile walk with an injured dog and hardly any supplies, in the middle of the rainy season. And he didn't know how far they were from the effects of the radiation. In the scheme of things, the cave didn't seem worth losing his life over, let alone his best friend. At this point there was no turning back. He didn't know what was left behind him. In the morning, they'd start their quest. From the mud-black depths of the ancient Nile, Alexander could hear the gargled singing: "'It's the end of the world as we know it.'" He shivered and pitched the tent.

Washington, DC

Under Mr. Stanley's command, the FVA took over the White House, and with it, the country. He was giving orders from the fallout shelter, which was fifty feet of lead and steel underneath Pennsylvania Avenue. The console he was sitting at was the back-up control system for the country's entire nuclear defense system.

Mr. Stanley watched the giant digital clock on the screen mounted into the wall tick down the final twenty minutes for the NOMAD system. All their efforts were put into keeping the missile launch systems going. There were decisions to be made, and it would take a great man, a courageous man. Mr. Stanley was always well-prepared. The last time his FVAs rebooted the NOMAD system, Mr. Stanley was able to decipher the presidential code for launching nuclear weapons. They were working on the second half of that code, which was held by the now-deceased secretary of defense.

As he watched his elite staff of programmers randomly generate access codes, seven out of the ten code numbers locked into place on the screen in front of him. He thought about his dad...eight numbers...he thought about pencil shavings...nine numbers...he thought about coffee stains...ten numbers.

Along the Nile, Sudan

Rebekah stared at the sky and whispered a quiet prayer. It was an awesome sight to see what man could create and destroy. The power of it was majestic; the horror of it was terrifying. They shielded their eyes from the bright light. This explosion was bigger than the previous one. Alexander still thought it was far enough away not to cause any radiation damage.

"I think Pandora's box has been opened. North Korea, China, Pakistan, and even India have nuclear weapons. Now they have found an excuse to use them," Rebekah said.

"We better start walking then," Alexander said.

"What about Bandit?" Rebekah looked at the dog, whose breathing was still labored.

"She's either going to have to walk or stay here," Alexander said, packing up their tent into the duffle bag.

"She saved your life," Rebekah protested.

"It's going to take everything we have to make it out of here. We have a long trek. No food, no water. We have to take care of ourselves first."

Rebekah knelt down next to Bandit and put her face into the dog's. The dog tried to wiggle her butt and groaned. Rebekah lifted one of her ears and said, "Come on, girl. It's time to go." The dog slowly got to her feet. With calculated steps, Bandit limped toward Alexander. Her breathing was short and quick, but her lungs sounded clear.

"The rib must be pressing against a lung, or maybe it's just bruised," Alexander said.

The rain tapered off. They followed the well-worn footpath that led from the Nile, as many people normally walked carrying water back to their village. The path was a hub of activity where people ran into friends and children played. Today it was empty. Just Rebekah, Alexander, and Bandit. Alexander took his compass out from the survival kit and pointed it southeast. They followed that path. Rebekah and Bandit followed him.

Alexander constantly looked back and forth, half expecting to see a snake crawl out across the mud path. He thought back about the cave and the spitting cobra and wondered how many were there. Rebekah trod carefully. He could feel her breath on his back. It wasn't a totally uncomfortable feeling, he thought. She was shadowing him as close as possible to avoid running into a snake. Alexander wished Amat was there to lead the way. The rain poured upon them. It wasn't a cool, refreshing rain, but a hot, steamy rain that added to the mud and the general feeling of discomfort. His jeans clung to him, and the mud had made them grow six inches taller. Poor Bandit was chest high, wading her way through the dark brown slush. He couldn't do anything for her or Rebekah.

He had never thought of himself as a hero type. More of a bookworm. He thought about his mom and nights on the back porch sipping lemonade and listening to bedtime stories in German, Russian, and Italian. His favorite was about a golden retriever that would jump into dreams and scare away monsters and bring children to safety. He turned around to see Bandit neck high in mud. She was standing still, her intelligent brown eyes staring at him. He thought about how brave the dog was and how she had rescued him. Now it was his turn. He made his way back to her and slung the old dog over his shoulders.

Rebekah smiled at the sight. She picked up the gear Alexander had been carrying and slung it over her shoulder.

They came to the edge of a village. A makeshift road had been cleared out along the grass. The village was empty. "We'll follow the road," Alexander said, holding the compass up into the air.

"I thought you said there were no roads," Rebekah said.

"A relief organization probably built this road between the village and their compound," Alexander explained. They walked through the village. As they walked, the horror of man overtook them. Rebekah wrinkled her nose at the stench of human waste, which assaulted her senses. It slapped her across the face.

Alexander looked around. Children's bodies were lying along the side of the road. The children were excited about visitors and must have run to greet their slayers. The bodies bore the marks of the crudely made machetes. He recognized some of the children as having been ones who had followed him and Amat around three months earlier. "What happened?" Rebekah asked.

Alexander caught the glint of a bead. He picked it up. It was a child's necklace, bearing the colors of a neighboring tribe. "It looks like the tribes are turning against each other," he said to Rebekah, feeling a slight chill as he remembered the prophecy.

"How do you know?"

"These beads are the colors of a neighboring tribe. We better hurry in case they are still here." Alexander did not relish the thought of dying miles from home. Especially because no one knew where they were. They reached the outskirts of the west side of the village; there, they found the body of one boy. His head was missing, but Alexander knew who he was. He was still holding a silver compass. Its dial was pointing west. He had been following the compass west to find help, which never came.

They came to the outskirts of the next village where they found an abandoned Jeep. Alexander walked over to it. He recognized the body in the driver's seat as an American agriculturist who worked for the relief organization. His hands and feet had been cut off. His throat was slit. He must have stopped to help in the village and been slaughtered.

"Why didn't they take the car?" Rebekah asked from over his shoulder.

"Many tribal Sudanese don't know how to drive." Alexander looked. The keys were dangling from the ignition.

"Why kill someone trying to help you?"

"His watch, shoes, and rings are gone. They must have wanted them." Alexander pulled the agriculturist's remains out of the vehicle. He took off his t-shirt and wiped the seats as best as he could. He placed Bandit in the back seat and tried to brace her ribs by using some of the gauze bandages in the survival kit. He also noticed there was an extra can of gas in the back. After Rebekah climbed into the passenger seat, Alexander steered the vehicle down the winding road, making sure they turned in a southeast direction. The rain stopped and the sun peeked out from the clouds.

"Maybe we are going to make it after all," Rebekah said, scratching at a sore that had appeared on the back of her hand.

"What's the last horror movie you saw?" Alexander asked, giving her a quick glance. She was accumulating sores down her bare-skinned arms.

"What do you mean?"

"That's the line that comes right before someone dies a horrible death."

Gunga Mountains, Sudan

The sizzle of something frying woke Amat up. He had slept well. He gave a great stretch and stepped out of the tent. Ariet was frying canned Spam on the fire. "Smells good," Amat said, using some of the purified water to wash his face.

Ariet was silent. "Did you sleep okay?" he asked. There was no answer.

"Breakfast is ready." She passed him a plate. They sat and ate breakfast in silence. The light drizzle turned into a heavy downpour. After eating, Amat packed up the tent while Ariet cleaned the cooking utensils. She was different from the night before. Amat didn't know if it was her resolve or if she had fallen off the edge. She was a very strong woman and could go either way.

"Breakfast was very good," he said, hoping to start some type of conversation.

"Thank you," came her short reply.

"The pass is approximately ten miles."

She didn't say anything. For the first two hours, they sloshed through the mud. It was uneventful. Ariet kept to herself. Amat hummed tunes in Swahili. This part of southern Sudan turned from a desert savanna to a lush jungle filled with miles of tall grass, plus the inescapable mud. So far no snakes. Amat cut their way through the elephant grass every few yards. Snakes did not like to be surprised and neither did Amat. In two days he had not seen a snake other than dead ones. In fact, he had seen three dead ones. He hadn't seen any animals like antelope or birds or mosquitoes. Flies were the national bird of Sudan, and he hadn't seen any of them either. He didn't like the look of it. His humming stopped. Things didn't seem normal. The sky lit up through the misty rain. At first, he thought it was lightning, but the entire sky flashed a brilliant white that rolled from the northeast, engulfing the horizon. Seconds later, the ground shook. The air seemed to suck in as if everything was caught in a vacuum. Ariet clung to Amat. Her eyes looked steadfastly in his as if seeking refuge.

"Watch your step," Amat said, stepping over three feet of a seven-foot python sticking out in the mud.

Ariet looked down and screamed. "It's dead," Amat said, grabbing her arm. As they looked around the clearing, they noticed everything was dead—birds, rats and snakes.

"What happened?" Ariet cringed at the devastating sight.

Amat bent down and looked at a rat lying in the path. There were open sores on its body. Its nose had oozed blood, and it was lying in its own vomit. He sighed. "What is it?" Ariet peered over his shoulder.

"I think some type of poisoning," he said, not wanting to tell her his worst fear. He wrinkled his brow. He had a feeling that it was radiation poisoning.

"What is going on?" Ariet crossed her arms over her breasts and shivered. She had never seen this type of devastation. It went on for what looked like miles. It seemed she and Amat were the only living, breathing creatures anywhere. This looked like a war zone. Except the maimed bodies were animals, not humans.

"We need to continue. We must make the pass." Amat took her hand and led her around the still bodies. She walked on tiptoes and stared at the ground so not to step on anything that once might have moved. She clung to Amat's hand. They walked in silence and could see the mountains in the distance. The rain increased. "We have to move faster if we want to make it," Amat said.

"What's the point?" Ariet tripped and fell onto her knees. She looked up at Amat, her eyes filled with tears. "That's it. I've had enough."

"What are you talking about? You can't give up now."

"There's nothing to go to. You saw the bombs. It's the end of the world. We might as well just sit here and die with the rest of the animals."

Amat put his hands under her armpits and pulled her up. "We're still alive. Isn't that enough? If we can get to the cave, we'll be okay. We'll make it. I promise you."

"And then what? There's nothing to go back to."

"Then we start over."

Ariet stared into his eyes for a long moment. She looked at the resolution and courage in them and longed to feel the same. They stood in the mud, the rain pouring around them. Her white dress was soaked and now stained with her father's blood and the deep mud that clung to everything. It clung to her skin. She didn't understand his urgency about reaching the cave, but she felt the urgency of his need. She believed in him. And that was enough for now. She held out her hand as a form of agreement. He took it, helped her rise up, and they walked on, hand in hand.

"You're not dead yet, and you're not an animal. If we can make it through the pass, we'll be safe in the caves. We'll be safe from any fallout. Believe in me," Amat said.

And she did.

They quickened their pace. "We can make the pass by nightfall, and we can make the cave in a day from there."

Ariet just smiled. The rain continued as they walked in silence. They passed a herd of rhinos. "See, we're not the only ones left," Amat told her. "It seems only the smaller animals were affected by the fallout."

"I'm glad we're not the only ones." She tried to add a little skip to her step.

By the time they reached the foothills of the Gunga Mountains and the base of the pass, it was late afternoon. In the summer, the pass was as wide as a city street. Now the constant rain and mudslides had reduced it to the size of a narrow gangway.

"Not much longer," Amat said as they entered the pass, which was surrounded by high cliffs on either side. "Watch out for the mudslides."

Normally it took Amat an hour to get to the valley. The mud and oozing slime from the sides made their path difficult. The path had narrowed from a hundred feet to five feet. They crept along. They were knee-deep in mud, and it didn't show any signs of letting up. If they didn't make it all the way, they could be buried in an avalanche of mud. Amat quickened his pace, pulling Ariet along. "Don't give up now," he encouraged her.

The Road to the Mountain, Sudan

The road twisted and turned through the wet, tall grass. Rebekah clung to the dashboard to keep her seat as she was jolted and jostled along. They slipped in the mud. As the twilight rolled in, they could barely make out the outline of the mountain range. The rain made it impossible to see where they were going, and Alexander was exhausted. They would have to stop for the night.

"Here, eat," Alexander said, handing her a granola bar. It was all he had been able to forage from Lloyd's kit.

She took one look at it, unrolled the window and threw up. The heaving continued even after her stomach was emptied. When she turned back to look at Alexander, her face was pale white and she was gasping for air. He touched her brow. She was on fire and shaking uncontrollably.

"It's radiation, isn't it?"

"No, I don't think so." Alexander didn't want to tell her the truth. After all, there was no recovery from radiation poisoning. She curled up in a ball. Bandit stuck her head through the armrest and licked Rebekah's face. Alexander covered her with a blanket and tried to get her to drink some water. He pulled her into his arms and held her through the night. He was unable to sleep. He kept watch, dozing occasionally and licking his puckered lips. He could still taste the lemonade on his father's back porch. He thought about the giant puzzle that was life. He thought about what Rebekah had said about the lexicon and how everything in the universe had a built-in shelf life. He thought about how fickle life was and what had brought him to this point in time. How could he put the pieces together? He remembered spending winter evenings in front of the fireplace with his mother, putting puzzles together. He thought about Father Paul standing by his mother's bedside, watching helplessly as she died. He thought about how God doesn't answer prayers. Bandit barked ferociously, breaking him from his trance. He saw the face of an Agunwi tribe member pounding on the driver's window. He was holding a machete.

"Oh, my God." Rebekah jolted upright, her eyes wide.

Alexander fumbled for the keys and started the ignition. Then he saw the blood streaking down the window. The native slid down the window, leaving a blurred red streak behind. Alexander recognized him as one of his frat brothers from his recent trip. He opened the door and stepped out next to the tribesman.

"What are you doing?" Rebekah reached out a hand to grab his arm.

"I know him. It's one of the men who worked with Amat and me." Bandit leapt to the front seat when Alexander dragged the tribesman into the back. Rebekah clung to the dog. The tribesman was wearing full Agunwi war gear. His face was streaked with blood-red stripes and he was wearing a loincloth. He shoulder was sliced open from a deep machete cut. Alexander grabbed the medicine bag. Donning gloves, he cleansed the wounds and bandaged it.

"What are you doing out here?" he asked.

"The tribes are fighting. It started when a goat was stolen. There is no stopping. No one will listen," the man said in halting English.

"Do you want to come with us? We're going to the Valley of the Voices," Alexander said.

The tribesman looked horrified. "No, you can't go there."

"We don't have any choice. It's the only place we'll be safe."

"Only medicine men can go there. No one has ever come back from there," the tribesman said.

"I have. I've been there."

He looked shocked and drew back from Alexander. "You've got demons." The tribesman jumped out of the vehicle and ran into the bush, wielding his machete. Moments later, the whole brush lit up like fireworks, and they could hear the staccato sounds of machine guns in the distance.

Alexander went to turn on the Jeep, and that's when he saw the approaching headlights from the Humvee. He grabbed Rebecca and called softly to the dog. He carried Rebekah into the brush. Alexander watched through the tall grass as the soldiers jumped out of their trucks. They shone their flashlights into the Jeep. Alexander could make out the uniforms of the LRA. He shuddered, remembering his last encounter with them.

Rebekah coughed. Alexander placed his hand gently over her mouth. She gasped for air and looked at him. "Becky, we have to be quiet," he whispered. Flashlights danced like fireflies through the tall grass as soldiers checked the perimeter, searching for other tribesmen. Alexander's heart pounded in his chest, wondering if he should stay still or if he should try to take them further away from the road. The Aussie watched intently, leaning closely against his back.

The commander of the soldiers whistled and signaled for the troops to head back into the transport. One of the soldiers jumped into the Jeep, following behind the Humvee. They headed into the night.

Alexander assessed the situation. There was no way they could walk through the brush at night, even if Rebekah had the strength. It was too dangerous. All his supplies were in the Jeep—all he had was the compass in his pocket, a flashlight, and the machete at his hip. The rain had lessened, and the sky was clearing. There was enough moonlight to see the area where they were hiding. The first thing Alexander had to do was get them off the ground—too many things moved in the night. Alexander wanted to get as far as possible from the worn path that they had been on. He scooped up Rebekah and headed into the tall grass, Bandit on his heels. After thirty minutes, he entered a grove of teak trees. He laid Rebekah down against a large tree. He thought it was safe to turn on the flashlight. The teak tree was larger than most, about five feet tall. It spread out several thick branches, making it a perfect spot to build his Swiss Family tree house for the night.

Alexander slashed at some smaller saplings until he had a good selection of fifteen or so to build the base for the tree house. He took some vines and tied them together, making a makeshift base and lined it with the soft grass. He built an A-frame and covered that with giant leaves that wouldn't hold during a downpour but might keep a drizzle out. He lifted Bandit into the tree house. "Becky," he whispered. Her eyes fluttered open slowly. "I'm going to have to lift you up into the tree," Alexander said.

Her body ached from the poison, and her skin burned. She knew she couldn't scream in case the soldiers were still near. Alexander lifted her into the tree house and followed behind her. He held her shaking body, trying to keep her warm. Bandit lay across her feet.

It was a fitful night. Alexander kept watch, alert to the sounds of the brush. The last time he had slept in the jungle, he was surrounded by buzzing flies and mosquitoes. He wondered why it was so quiet. Before, the jungle came alive at night. He thought about the tree house that he and his dad had built in his back yard. They made a blueprint out of drawings from the Swiss Family Robinson book. He wondered how his dad was doing and wished he could send him a picture of this tree house. He fought hard to stay awake, but he was physically and emotionally exhausted. Alexander felt himself drifting off and tried to wake himself with a jerk. That's when he heard Bandit's low growl. "What's wrong, girl?" Alexander asked, startled from his sleep. He looked around. Even with the dim moonlight, he couldn't see anything but tall grass. He turned on the flashlight and couldn't make out anything until the light caught in the reflection of a pair of almond-shaped eyes, not more than fifty feet away.

Bandit got up. Her gaze intensified and she barked. "Easy girl," he said, trying to quiet her down. From his jungle training, he knew not to make any quick movements. He hadn't seen many animals over the last few days. If this was a cat, it would be hungry or injured and even more dangerous. He reached down for his machete. Bandit leapt out of the tree house. She stumbled once she landed before taking off into the tall grass. Alexander yelled after her, but it was too late. He jumped out of his shelter, machete in one hand.

Bandit's barking was answered by a lion's roar. Alexander's heart stilled. He couldn't leave Rebekah, nor could he help Bandit. Looking at the sleeping Rebekah, he decided to chance it and took off in the brush after Bandit. He followed the trampled grass, where he found Bandit standing over the body of the lioness. She was covered in open sores, lying next to her two dead cubs. Bandit sat silent, staring at the lioness. They shared a look of understanding. She was just protecting her cubs. Alexander could feel that Bandit understood. The dog looked up at him and slowly walked back to the tree house.

The sun rose. Alexander climbed as high as he could to the top of the tree to get a better view. From his high perch, he could see the Gunga Mountains couldn't be more than seven miles away. The Jeep was gone. It didn't matter either way. There were no roads from this point leading into the valley. He could see the glistening water of the Nile, not more than a half mile away. The Nile was the DMZ no-man's land of Sudan.

He looked down at Rebekah, who stirred. She was in no shape to walk the seven miles to the valley. As he climbed down, she woke up. She managed a smile as she watched him shimmy down the tree like a twelve-year-old boy in his backyard. It looked like he was having fun.

"How you feeling?" Alexander asked.

"I feel better. I really needed to sleep." Rebekah sat up. "I'm actually hungry."

Alexander said. "How do you feel about fish for breakfast? I've got a plan."

Washington, DC

The hood covering Colonel Talcott's head smelled strongly of disinfectant. He couldn't tell how long he'd been out. His chest still ached from where the taser hit him. Through the darkness, he tried to feel his surroundings. His arms were handcuffed behind him to a hard chair. He tried to struggle but couldn't get free. He could hear the steady hum of an air conditioning vent and not much more. He knew no matter what happened next, the end result would be the same—he'd be dead. Even knowing this fact, he remained calm. His many years as a soldier both on and off the field gave him the inner peace to not fear death.

A door opened and the smell of disinfectant grew stronger. Mr. Stanley walked into the room. He pulled the hood off Colonel Talcott and pulled up another steel chair so he was sitting directly in front of him. Mr. Stanley kept a safe distance from his prisoner.

Mr. Stanley was wearing a perfectly tailored suit with a little blue NATO pin on his lapel. His hands were covered in latex gloves. He thought the uniform was appropriate for the man who was cleansing the world; plus, he didn't have to wash his hands nearly as much if he kept the gloves on.

"Colonel Talcott, do you know who I am?" he asked.

The colonel blinked a few times, adjusting his eyes to the single halogen light that hung from the center of the room. He knew who Mr. Stanley was but didn't say a word.

"Sorry about the handcuffs and the situation you're in right now," Mr. Stanley said. "I'd hoped you would help us willingly. You're a colonel in the US Army. I would think you'd want to help your country."

"This isn't my country anymore," Colonel Talcott spat out.

"If you don't care about your county anymore, perhaps you care about your son," Mr. Stanley said.

"Sonofabitch, what have you done?" Colonel Talcott muttered through gritted teeth and struggled to free his arms.

"I sent a SEAL team to Sudan to make sure your son and Rebekah Simmonds are safely brought back home. I need you to talk to your son and let him know we all want him to come home safely. There's a place in our new government for him and Rebekah and for you, Colonel Talcott, if you choose to cooperate." Mr. Stanley rubbed his hands together. "I have nothing against you or your son. I just need the girl and what's she is carrying. It's essential for the survival of our country."

Colonel Talcott smiled at Mr. Stanley, not speaking.

Mr. Stanley scooted his chair closer to the Colonel and smiled back. "I didn't think so." Mr. Stanley got up and walked behind the chair where Colonel Talcott was sitting. The colonel could smell the gasoline as it poured down his head and neck, soaking his clothes. It burned his eyes, and he closed his mouth. He closed his eyes tightly. Colonel Talcott thought about his first day at boot camp and the pride he felt donning the army green for the first time.

He thought about Kuwait and the burning oil fields. The hot desert sand and the occasional cold beer at night, sitting around with his fellow soldiers, some of them who never made it back. He thought about a beautiful young Irish girl with flaming red hair and laughing green eyes, whose skin smelled like moonbeams and magnolia. He thought about an eight-year-old boy up in a tree house in the backyard. He knew that boy would be okay. When he opened his eyes, Mr. Stanley stood in front of him, flicking open a solid gold Zippo lighter embossed with the numbers 451.

When he ignited the flame, Colonel Talcott broke his thumb on his right hand, enabling him to slip his hand out of the handcuffs and in one motion grab Mr. Stanley, pulling him in tightly as the two were engulfed in flames.

Sudan

The Nile stretched wide, gushing from the recent constant rains. The water pushed back against the foliage surrounding it, making it green and lush, unlike the brown and dusty ground Alexander had seen months before. The volcanic silt rushed down the Blue Nile, making the valley an oasis in an otherwise barren land. As Alexander took in the sight, he thought about the cradle of civilization, how this would be the perfect birthplace for man. He grabbed a beetle and hooked it to his emergency kit fishing line. He deposited it into the river and squatted, waiting patiently for breakfast.

Bandit followed behind him and sat watching. Rebekah watched the two as she leaned against a teak tree. She felt remarkably better after getting restful sleep.

The fishing line slowly straightened and then tugged. Alexander pulled in a nice size catfish. The three devoured their breakfast, Bandit not stopping to chew.

"Rebekah, do you feel strong enough to continue on?" Alexander asked.

"Alex, I don't think we have a choice. We have to keep moving," she said.

Alexander collected up fallen teak logs and tied them together with vines. All he needed was something that could take them the six or seven miles down the river, bringing them close enough to the valley entrance. Three months ago, he and Amat would never have taken the river as it would have been too narrow, and it would have made them a target for the northern Sudanese. He gathered up their few remaining supplies and helped Rebekah onto the raft as Bandit sat watching. Australian shepherds did not like water, period. She had jumped in to save Alex, but short of that, there was no way she was getting on the raft.

Alexander took out the last remaining piece of beef jerky from his kit. "C'mon, girl, it's going to be okay." He held out the beef jerky, trying to lure the dog onto the raft. She sat back watching him with a stubborn headshake. "Fine, have it your way." He stomped through the water, picked up the sixty-five-pound dog and carried her to the raft. Putting her down, she stood in the dead center of the raft. Alexander pushed off the shore with his makeshift paddle. The current quickly took them downriver. They passed much of the same lush scenery. It would be a pleasant journey if not for the reason for it.

As they rounded a bend, the raft hit a bump, tossing Bandit into the water. Alexander flew to the other side of the raft, reaching in after her, almost toppling over everything. He managed to grab her by the neck. She was frantic, panicking. The bump they hit raised its head. A Nile hippopotamus chomped at Bandit, barely missing her. Alexander hit the hippo with his paddle and grabbed the dog. The hippopotamus went under the water. Rebekah screamed, "Alex, he's coming after us."

Rebekah picked up the other paddle and the two swiftly paddled as quickly as they could. Her arms ached and she coughed. The current picked up, turning the muddy water into whitecap rapids. Bumping off rocks, the raft started to tear apart. Rebekah held onto the shaking Aussie as Alexander tried to pilot their way through the rushing water.

As the mountains that separated Sudan from Ethiopia appeared around the bend, the rapids turned to a steady slow flow. Alexander pushed their way to the shore. The three collapsed, breathing heavily. Bandit shook the water off her fur and butted her head against Alexander.

In the Mountain Pass, Sudan

What little light was left through the rain was given them by Amat's flashlight. They could barely see more than a few feet in front of them. It was hard to tell rain from mud. The light from the flashlight bounced off the cliffs. There was no turning back; either they would make it or not. They had given up trying to talk as the rain and narrow passageway made them walk single file.

"How much farther?" Ariet screamed, trying to be heard over the thunder and torrential rain.

His instinct told him they were at least halfway, before the lightning struck and he could make out the outline of a clearing. "Not too much. I can see just ahead," he said, grabbing her hand and pulling her through the mud. Each time the lightning exploded across the sky, he turned and looked, and he could see her determined face. She had reached the crossroads between hope and despair and had chosen hope. Her eyes were clear and focused. She didn't have that lost look. It renewed his faith.

She now walked beside him as she leveraged herself through the mud. Amat had thought they had another hour to go. But the hour turned into four. As they trudged through the mud, sometimes slipping back two steps for every one forward, their heels grew four inches as the mud caked to the bottom of their feet. Their legs ached from the strain. It seemed like it would be forever. And then they entered the clearing. Ariet sank down onto the wet grass, the rain pouring down around her.

"We made it," she said.

Amat knelt down beside her, pulling her into his arms. "Yes, we did." He kissed her lightly on her lips. And then again. The rain let up. The sky turned to a grayish white. A hazy film rode up to meet the sky. It was hard to catch their breaths in the hot muggy air with the mildew.

The clearing was just a clearing lined with short grass, giggle weed, and thorn brush. No trees. It was at the mouth of the mountain pass. It was hard to see past this plateau, but the ground rose steadily. It seemed that the valley was safe from the fallout. There were plenty of mosquitoes and flies, which also meant there were plenty of snakes. Ariet was exhausted. They climbed to the entrance of the valley and then they had to rest. Amat set up their tent to escape the flies and mosquitoes, but what worried him more were the snakes. The next two miles would be an easy walk. However, all their energy had fled them. As the sun cleared away, polishing the sky, he was amazed to see the river of mud they had crossed. Another couple of days of rain and the pass would be closed off. They'd be safe from the world.

Ariet was fast asleep. Amat woke up to the sound of birds chirping, the buzzing of flies, and the rushing of water. He was amazed at how beautiful the valley looked, especially compared to the harsh Sudan desert. He thought about his days with the Catholic missionaries and wondered if this was what the Garden of Eden must have looked like—a lush refuge in the heart of darkness.

In the distance he saw smoke rising up at the beginning of the pass. He grabbed his machete and field glasses. He motioned to Ariet to stay down, not wanting to give away their presence.

He lifted the field glasses up to his eyes. Looking though them, he made out two faint figures and what appeared to be a dog, perched around a fire. He worked his way along the ridge, not wanting to be seen to get a closer look. He looked through the field glasses again and made out the face of his friend.

"My friend," Amat called, waving his arms and sloshing through the mud toward Alexander. His words were lost in the rush of the water cascading down the mountainside.

Alexander looked up to see a figure struggling toward him. In the distance, he could not make out who it was. It was an hour before the figure was close enough to make out who it was: a tall, black man. With a slow hand so as not to be seen, Alexander reached for his machete. Bandit drew to attention at Alexander's side and let out a low growl.

As the figure got closer, Alexander recognized his old friend. "Amat," he called out.

"My friend," Amat called back. With long strides, Amat quickly closed the space that separated them.

Bandit circled Amat, sniffing. Amat backed off. "Don't be afraid. She's harmless," Alexander said, patting the brave dog.

"How'd you get here?" Amat asked.

The two shared stories of their journey as they sat by the fire. "This is my friend, Rebekah," Alexander said.

Amat could see the sores on her face and arms and knew what had caused them. This was not good. "Hello," he said, putting out his hand. "It is so nice to meet you."

Rebekah smiled. "I've heard so much about you, and I've seen the pictures." She sat down next to Alexander. The river had zapped the last of her strength. "I need to see the cave Alexander has told me about. I need to see these drawings in person."

"It's not much further. I'll show you." Amat stood up.

As Rebekah started to stand, her legs gave. She slid back onto the ground.

"Rebekah," Alexander yelled in concern, reaching down to help steady her. Looking over to Amat, he said, "I don't think she can make the walk."

"I think any more days of rain and none of us will make it back to the valley, my friend," Amat said. Alexander held Rebekah while Amat gathered materials to build a stretcher. He cut down two large saplings to make poles and then laced it with vines and elephant ear leaves.

Alexander placed Rebekah on the rough stretcher, putting the backpack under her head for a pillow. The two men each took an end. With Amat leading the way, they walked through the mud and valley. Bandit followed behind, chest-high in the mud, trying her best to keep up.

Even though the rain had stopped, there was still a steady flow of water off the canyon walls, making it slippery and hard to walk. By the time they reached the valley, Ariet had a fire going with boiling water to drink. She had gathered some plantains and mangoes. They all sat and ate while Amat introduced Ariet and told the story of the riots in Nairobi and their journey to the valley. No one talked about the mushroom clouds they all had seen.

And then Amat asked, "What's going on with the rest of the world?"

"Did you see the explosions?" Alexander asked.

"Yes, and I saw many dead animals along the trail." He looked down at Bandit, who was lying at his feet. The Aussie did not seem affected except for a bandaged leg.

Alexander rubbed the sore on his hand. "Yes, I'm afraid we may have been too close to the fallout."

"The important thing is you are both alive," Amat said, thinking of Oleg and Stan.

"I wouldn't call this living, but I guess you're right," Alexander answered, thinking of Lloyd and wondering if his dad was safe.

"What's our next step?" Amat asked.

Alexander looked around the fire at Ariet, at Amat, and finally at Rebekah, whose face was covered with sores. At least now she could hold her head up and carry her weight. The meager food seemed to have revived her. "I think we head to the caves. At least we'll be protected if another bomb goes off," Alexander said.

They gathered their few belongings and headed to the cave. "This should be an easier route. It's about two miles," Amat said, pointing to a trail.

After a half hour, they noticed a crudely made hut by the side of the mountain. "I don't remember seeing that last time we were here," Alexander said.

"It wasn't here when I returned with my team either," Amat agreed with Alexander. "Let's stop."

The group stopped and watched as an old man came out to greet them with a young boy beside him. Amat recognized them to be the medicine man of Odella and his grandson, Kuot. The medicine man smiled a toothless grin. The boy brought antelope skins out for them to sit on. They sat under a tree to avoid the rain, which had started up again.

Amat introduced everyone and explained they were seeking refuge in the cave and wanted to see the drawings once again.

"My grandson and I left Odalla when the killing started. No one dared follow us into the valley," Amat translated the medicine man's story. "There is no safe place anymore. Even the Valley of the Voices has lost its power. The spirits have gone. Soon the whole sky will be on fire again."

"What do you mean?" Amat asked at Alexander's request.

"The voices of the cave tell about the glowing sky and the end of all being."

"Is he talking about the apocalypse?" Rebekah asked.

"Many cultures have revelations about the end of the world. I've never heard one from Africa," Amat replied.

The medicine man sent the boy into the hut. He came out with an antelope skin wrapped and tied around something. The old man opened it. He passed his hand over it as if to bless it and muttered something. He revealed the seventh scroll, which appeared similar to the ones Amat had been carrying.

"This one has only been seen by the keepers of the cave. My father, my grandfather, and his grandfather before him. All my ancestors were great medicine men," the boy translated for his grandfather. "I was handing it down to my grandson when his father was killed. It became his legacy. Now I'm afraid he'll never get to keep it."

As the old man pointed out the story on the scroll and talked, it was obvious without deciphering that it told of great destruction and rebirth. As they talked, Rebekah examined the drawings on the scroll.

Amat translated for the holy man. "The great being sent the rains to cleanse the world from the evil people. This is when the rain beetles were everywhere. When the rain stopped, the earth was new and the people all gathered to live together. They all spoke one language and were filled with power." Amat paused to think of how to translate the African word. He continued, "They built a tower to reach the skies. The great being was not pleased with their pride and made them confused."

"He's talking about the Tower of Babel," Alexander interrupted. "According to Genesis, after the great flood, the Canaanites became a powerful urbanized society. They built the Tower of Babel out of baked bricks as a testimony to their skills and their technology."

Rebekah interrupted. "In his wisdom, God knew their stairway to heaven would lead them away from him." She examined the scroll. A drawing of a cobra with the chaotic myth symbol on its hood was wrapped around a tree. She looked up from the drawing. The tree they were sitting under resembled the one in the drawing. Above the devastation a circle shaped shadow eclipsed the sun. They stared at the scroll in silence, not believing what they saw.

"According to the Bible, God sent the rains to cleanse the world, he destroyed the Tower of Babel, he sent Moses the commandments, and finally he sent his son who we crucified. All because we strayed away from God. Each time, the world kept just enough of the original voice of God to keep the world from ending, but now we've gotten bigger than God. We can't talk in the old language anymore," Rebekah said, holding onto her cross. "In this scroll, it shows how each civilization, as it advanced, reached a certain stage of enlightenment and then destroyed itself. The snake represents the knowledge of evil."

Alexander interrupted her. "By listening to the snake, Eve dared to disobey God, dared to ask 'What if?' What if man was equal to God? We've done the same with our pursuit of knowledge and the information highway. The Internet is our Tower of Babel."

"How did the world survive all these devastations?" Amat asked the medicine man.

"We kept the voice," the old man said simply. "The Great Being spoke to us in the old language from the sky. His great beam of light cleansed the earth."

"Who is the Great Being?" Alexander asked.

A bomb blew up. The white light brightened the sky and the now-familiar gray mushroom cloud followed it.

"They're getting closer," Amat said.

"We should head for the cave. Ask him if we can take the scroll," Alexander said, standing up.

Amat asked and the medicine man nodded. The boy rewrapped the scroll and handed it to Amat with a flourish. "Will you come along?" Amat asked.

"He says he's too old, but I should go," the boy replied. They bid their farewell to the old man, who handed them some food wrapped in a cloth.

Alexander pointed to the entrance of the mountains. "Can you make it?" he asked Rebekah.

She looked up at the mountain, took a deep breath, and nodded her head.

The old man disappeared into the hut and came out with a red gas can with the words "World Relief" stenciled on the side. He handed it Amat.

"What's that for?" Alexander asked.

"It's for our new home," Amat replied.

"What does he mean?" Rebekah asked.

"Snakes," was all Alexander said with a shudder.

After gathering their supplies, they started the slow trek uphill. The rains had made the climb slippery, but the lush greenery kept the soil intact. The cave was on the east ridge of the mountain, which was covered with foliage.

When they reached the mouth of the cave, there didn't seem to be as many snakes as Amat had thought or remembered. At least not live ones. The radiation was not strong enough to be lethal to humans, but it had helped with the snake population. The Aussie, having three times the stamina of an average dog, seemed untouched and her leg was healing. There were dead rats and snakes, but the cockroaches were doing well. They seemed quite happy. The floor was a carpet of frenzied cockroaches.

Rebekah hesitated going in. "It doesn't get much better, Beck," Alexander said.

She nodded and took his hand. When she first saw the drawings on the wall, she stopped and lightly touched them as though they were the Holy Grail. "You can feel the power of these."

"Wait here," Amat said as he ran down the corridor with his flashlight and the gasoline.

Rebekah's foot slid on something. She screamed and dug her nails into Alexander's arm. "It's okay. It's a dead snake," Alexander said, shining his flashlight on the floor of the cave.

Amat came back. They could see smoke behind him. "We should go out in the fresh air for a while," he said. They went and sat on the ridge near the cave. Snakes slithered out. Amat nailed them with his machete. Africans hate snakes. If the radiation and gasoline didn't get every snake within ten miles, Amat was determined he would. After the fire had died down, he led them to the inner cave, showing them the way over the secret bridge, which crossed the pit still glowing from fire. The smell of gasoline mixed with the smoke and the burning flesh of the snakes was more than Rebekah could take. She fell to her knees and lost the little lunch she had kept down.

Alexander stared in awe when they entered the inner cave. "This is more incredible than the pictures," he said.

The walls of the cave were painted with pictures that matched the ones on the seventh scroll, depicting a cobra wrapped around a tower. On the back of the cobra's head was the chaotic math symbol.

"This is just like the scroll. It's telling the story of the Tower of Babel," Alexander said. "This is why we couldn't decipher the words. They're a combination of all different languages."

He walked around and studied the pottery and the tools. "These are all from Mesopotamia. About 6,000 years ago. Bible scholars date the Tower of Babel to 4,000 BC. These people must have fled the genocide. Israelites killed all the Canaanites."

Amat nodded his head in agreement. "These are our ancestors, Ariet. From these people came all the nations of the world," Amat said. "In southern Africa, they became the Nubians, in the north, the Egyptians. Across the sea, they became the Arabs."

"The skeletons are...unsettling..." Ariet shuddered and looked away.

"Don't look away. These are brave souls who gave their lives so civilization could go on," Amat said, putting his arm around her shoulder.

"Now it's our turn," Alexander said.

"I've been looking at this seventh scroll," Rebekah said. "According to the scrolls, they could no longer talk in their father's language."

"In Hebrew? In Aramaic?" Alexander asked with a wrinkled brow.

"You remember when we first put the drawings in the correlator it described how the scribes of these drawings talked about blood knowledge—how it's not a magical howl at the moon but a practical scientific blueprint to who they are," Rebekah paused, then continued. "We thought they were talking about DNA as we know it, but they were talking about the original lexicon."

"What are you saying, Becky?"

"This last tribe knew how to talk to God. They left us the secret. It was a warning. It's in the Koran, the Bible, the Talmud. In the beginning was the word. We are the word."

"You mean we have to remember how to talk to God?" Amat asked.

"You mean like 'our father,' like prayer?" Alexander asked.

"I'm sure that people are praying all over the world right now. It's not working," Rebekah said. She let out a big sigh and collapsed.

Alexander ran to her side and put her head on his lap. "Are you all right?"

"I don't want to die in here," Rebekah said, her voice barely above a whisper.

Alexander scooped her up. Holding her, he stood in front of Amat, Ariet, Kuot, and Bandit. He looked around at his friends. "Amat, you are now the last tribe," he said.

Rebekah whispered to Alexander. He reached inside her backpack and pulled out the correlator drive. He handed it to Amat. "This drive will help you start over, if that's how you choose to go. I don't know what's right. I don't know how God wants us to start again. I don't even know if there is a God," Alexander said.

Amat hugged him and kissed Rebekah. "God will be with you, my friends."

With one last look behind him, Alexander turned and carried Rebekah over the bridge and out of the cave with Bandit close behind.

Ariet and Amat watched their friends leave the cave. "We should go with them," Ariet said, following Alexander's path.

"It's not safe for us to go out yet," Amat said, grabbing her arm to hold her back.

"Will it ever be safe for us again?" she asked.

Amat took her in his arms and stared deeply into her eyes. "I promise you that, whatever happens, we will go through this together."

When Alexander and Rebekah exited the cave, they saw the valley was engulfed in flames. Bandit took a step back before steadying herself and following them out of the cave.

"We have to go higher," Alexander said, looking down at the spreading fire.

Rebekah's nosebleed was constant now. She repeatedly murmured the words to the Lord's Prayer in a whisper. Cradling her in his arms, Alexander started the slow climb. What once was lush green mountainside was singed, smoldering and black. He looked down at Rebekah. She was getting worse; the red of her nose made the pallor of her skin stand out. He just knew if they stopped they would die, so he kept moving despite the aching in his legs and strain on his arms.

The climb was treacherous, but at least it wasn't steep. Rebekah's breathing became more labored the higher they climbed and the thinner the air became. Her murmurings had become more strained. The east ridge of the mountain range stood a thousand feet over the cave. Bordering the mountain on the other side was Ethiopia. When they reached the top, Alexander scanned the landscape. What they saw was complete and utter destruction. Flames as far as the eyes could see. The distant mushroom cloud filled the sky with smoke. It rolled over the sun like a thick blanket of death. Alexander looked for somewhere to ride out the smoke.

Rebekah collapsed in his arms. "Alexander, I'm so scared. Not just for me but for our world. I'm afraid that the world is dying with me. I feel so helpless."

Alexander drew her closer, trying to shield her from the smoke. "Everything we know from history, religion," his throat burning from the smoke and ash as he talked, "the world goes on, we go on."

"God spoke to Abraham, to Moses, to all the saints and martyrs," Rebekah whispered, choking back a cough. "They heard his voice; Adam and Eve walked with God and knew him. How did they talk with God? Where is he now? How can he let this happen?"

Standing up on top of the ridge, Alexander looked around. Rebekah coughed. Alexander tightened his arms around her.

She looked at him with tears in her eyes. "'In the beginning there was the word and the word was God.'"

Alexander shook his head. She coughed harder and spoke in a whisper. "'And God created the heavens and the earth. All the creatures in the sea and on land. Then he created man in his own image.' How did Adam and Eve communicate with God before they ate from the tree of knowledge? They walked with God. All they knew was God."

When Alexander looked down at Rebekah, her eyes were closed. He shook her. "Becky, don't go." He kissed her. Her lashes fluttered open. With a hoarse voice, Rebekah said, "God is speaking to us; we're not listening."

He could feel Rebekah's life slipping away in his hands. He knelt on the ground, cradling her. He looked to heaven, not sure what to say or do. He instinctively shut down and at the same time opened up. As he let go of this world, he opened up to another. A surge of electricity exploded as millions of synapses ignited at once. His whole body became a receiver. Every part of him became a receptacle. In that moment he understood. The voice of God, our shared lexicon, was not spoken; it was in our blood, encrypted in our DNA. As children of God, we carried his bloodline. After millennia of natural selection, we lost that one nucleotide, that single part of the chemical puzzle that connected us as a species to our creator and to each other. The Garden of Eden wasn't a place, it was a state of mind. All we knew was God until we asked the one forbidden question: what if? What if we dare disobey Him? We traded faith for knowledge and stretched the rubber band too far. Now it had snapped back. All our technology, our false idols, couldn't save us from ourselves. The sky grew darker, thick from the smoke. Alexander collapsed next to Rebekah.

A bright light crashed across the sky. For a moment, time stood still. Alexander watched as the smoke parted and the sun was eclipsed. A shadow crossed between the earth and the rest of the universe. A gentle rain fell on them. For a moment he could catch his breath. The soft rain turned into a downpour, cleansing the scorched earth around them and putting out the smoldering fires. Alexander felt the warmth from the light. A second surge of light, more intense than the first, filled the air with the smell of ozone. Alexander felt the light embrace him, his body shook.

It was easier to breathe. He held Rebekah and kissed her softly.

Her eyes opened as she gasped for air. "Alex, I heard his voice, not in words but in images, images of a new world." Her breathing was less labored.

Alexander managed a smile. "Becky, I thought I lost you."

The rain was cool and soothing to their skin. The air was cleaner, purified. The burning in their lungs subsided. Rebekah sat up. "His voice spoke from within me." She began crying.

Alexander kissed her face. The lesions were gone, washed away. "Your face, your beautiful face! Becky?"

Rebekah held on to Alexander's arm and slowly stood up. She looked around, taking in the view. "I don't understand Alex, I was gone. I felt transparent, without substance. I could see you, I could see you holding me." She hugged him.

"Let's get out of the rain." Alexander said.

As they made their way back to the cave, the rain stopped and a rainbow appeared over the valley. From the dust of the Earth, man was made again. A new covenant would begin.

In loving memory of Bandit

About the Author

An award-winning journalist for the *Chicago Tribune*, Vicki Vass' travels in southern Sudan inspired the story behind Eleven: 1. While there covering the civil war, she learned from her guide, Amat, a Sudanese history professor, that there are more than 365 languages in southern Sudan. Due to the difficulty in traveling between villages, each tribe has developed its own language. This led to her ask the question: What is the original language of man and what happens when we forget it?

Vicki is a perilous antique hunter braving the world of bargains to curate stories for her cozy mystery series, *Antique Hunters Mystery* also available on vickivass.com and Amazon.com.

She has an Australian shepherd named Bandit, who is smarter than her and appears in every book.

www.ingramcontent.com/pod-product-compliance
Lightning Source LLC
Chambersburg PA
CBHW030327130626
46554CB00011B/191